S H E L L E Y   J A C K S O N

The Melancholy of Anatomy

Shelley Jackson was born in the Philippines, grew up in Berkeley, studied art at Stanford and writing at Brown, and now lives in Brooklyn. She is the author of *Patchwork Girl,* a hypertext novel.

THE
MELANCHOLY
OF
ANATOMY

To Steve

THE MELANCHOLY OF ANATOMY

at Lake Forest, 2006
with steaming puddles of a nameless fluid —

Stories

SHELLEY JACKSON

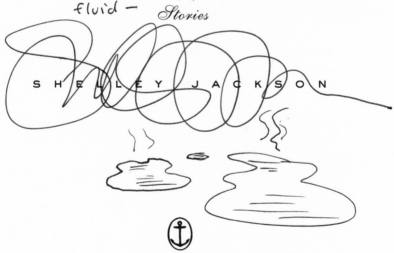

Anchor Books

A DIVISION OF RANDOM HOUSE, INC.

NEW YORK

First Anchor Books Edition, March 2002

Library of Congress Cataloging-in-Publication Data

Jackson, Shelley.
The melancholy of anatomy : stories / Shelley Jackson.
p. cm.
ISBN 0-385-72120-X
1. Body, Human—Fiction. I. Title.

PS3560.A2448 M45 2002
813'.54—dc21
2001055329

Anchor ISBN: 0-385-72120-X

Author photo © Sylvia Plachy

www.anchorbooks.com

Printed in the United States of America
10 9 8 7 6 5 4 3 2 1

For Wesley

CONTENTS

HEART

3

Choleric

EGG

9

SPERM

37

FOETUS

45

Melancholic

CANCER

57

NERVE

69

DILDO

82

Phlegmatic

PHLEGM
93

HAIR
124

SLEEP
127

Sanguine

BLOOD
137

MILK
156

FAT
167

THE
MELANCHOLY
OF
ANATOMY

HEART

There are hearts bigger than planets: black hearts that absorb light, hope, and dust particles, that eat comets and space probes. Motionless, sullen dirigibles, they hang in the empty space between galaxies. We can't see them, but we know they're there, fattening.

They give off a kind of light, but it is a backwards light that races inward away from the onlooker to hide itself from view, so this light, whose color we would so much like to know (maybe it's a color we haven't seen before, for which we must sprout new eyes), looks more like darkness than any ordinary darkness, and seems to suck the sight from our eyes, and make itself visible in the form of a blind spot.

Dark hearts, heavier than weight itself. Too heavy for reality to bear, they punch a hole in it, and sink through into the dream underneath. They throb dully at the bottom of a gravity well. We might sit by the side and drop a line, if we knew what kind of bait to use, but if we hooked the heart, could we lift it? And if the melancholy behemoth sounded of its own accord, bothered by our flies and sinkers, and we netted it, wouldn't it collapse on the deck, exhausted by its own gravity?

No, it is unkind to wrest these hearts out of hiding. Toss pennies in the hole, instead. Dump a martini off the poop of the spaceship, blow a kiss through a porthole and clear off, friend.

The heart warps everything around it. Where nothing is, emptiness itself is twisted, its features distorted beyond all recognition. This is why people rail against the heart. It is bad enough to change everything that is, but when nothingness itself is altered, something must be done.

If we hold ourselves still, at the moment the year turns over, we can feel a faint beat. That is the black heart continuing its patient, serious work. What work? I am trying to find out. I have given my life to observing the hearts. Observing, of course, is the wrong word for the patient cultivation of blind spots, for trying to understand, by the ways in which, yes, I do *not* understand, what the heart is. In this investigation, invisibility is evidence, blindness the closest I may come to insight, the particular shape and tenor of ignorance, a clue and a scripture. When I can no longer see anything, I will know I am face to faceless with the heart. What, I sit at my telescope, straining my neck, my fingers numb claws, in hopes of catching sight of nothing at all? Yes. I will know it when I don't see it.

Is it right to call by the same name the tiny, ruby red "hearts" children dig up in the garden? Those rubbery knots, the size of crab apples, that bounce so high but so erratically, shoot off in unexpected directions, are forever being fished from under sofas and on top of bookshelves? That let out a squeak when rubbed? It's true that as they roll through the strict formations—parallel lines, rings, spirals—of children's games they sometimes resemble gay little planets, comets, and asteroids. But where is the pity, the mystery in these toys?

I do know of a rare game played in certain valleys in the Appalachians (its reach is tied to the vicissitudes of one or two family lines) in which one piece is chosen by lot as the Black Heart and plays a different role in the game than the others. As in other games, you must win as many hearts as you can. You must not take the Black Heart, however, or all the points you have won count against you. If you capture it by accident, you must try to force someone else to take it from you.

There is one other strategy. If, at the end of the game, you have lost all your hearts, including your shooter, and hold only the Black Heart in your pot, you collect all the hearts everyone else has won. A dangerous way to win, to seek a perfect loss. I have come to look on this game as a parable, in which all the secrets of the Black Heart are revealed.

CHOLERIC

E G G

Part One

My name is Imogen. I am thirty-six. I live in a pretty, disintegrating apartment on the Mission/Castro divide with my roommate, Cass, with whom I have, as they say, "a history." I work in an upscale organic grocery store, where I restock toothpaste, candles, hand-carved wooden foot-rollers. I use Crest and buy candles cheap at Walgreens, but I like to look at the jewellike soap we sell, and the girls who finger it while gazing somewhere else entirely, as if waiting for a sign. I rarely speak to them. I'm not like them: they are sincere, optimistic, gentle. Sometimes they flirt with me, their open faces radiant and slightly spotty, their new piercings inflamed, but I have little will to carry things further. I have been "between" girlfriends for two years. I have my pride, and my disappointments. I'm not giving these details because I think they are interesting, but in order to mortify my own urge to simplify, to invent answers and then "find" them—like plucking an Easter egg out of the bush where I myself hid it an hour before.

An Easter egg, how droll.

READING NOTES, JUNE 14

Nothing is more ordinary than the egg: its likeness appears in the painted hands of kings and saints, under the paws of stone lions, bouncing across ballfields. Yet nothing is more mysterious. People used to believe the toad lived far underground, encased in rock, and that inside the toad's head was a lump of gold. That gold is the egg: locked, rumored, precious.

I now look upon the day the egg arrived as the most unfortunate of my life. I did not see it this way at the time; then, the egg seemed like the culmination of a long, confused, but fairly steady progress, which required only that punctuation to make sense. Like everyone I knew, I had always thought I would do something more important later on. Now later on had come. How stupid I was!

Had I been happy before then? I would scarcely have said so. I was restless and often embittered by this or that nuisance of my everyday life—my coworker Marty, the meter maid with a grudge against me, the band (Joss Stick) that practiced in the apartment beneath me, afternoons.

Yet I think I *was* happy. The world seemed open at the edges, fenceless. I smiled, I complained, I ate a veggie burger, I was more or less what I seemed to be, and now I suspect this was happiness.

Then the egg was lowered in front of me, like bait.

READING NOTES, JUNE 17

The egg eats. At least, it swallows things. You can watch them being expelled later. At first they are just shadows. Then they have color as well, and can be felt through the wall of the egg, like new teeth. Finally, only a tight skin like a balloon's covers the object, now perfectly visible. This splits and curls back, and the object falls outside the egg.

These discards do not seem damaged, but they are. They are different afterwards, like food laid out for fairies: it's still there in the morning, but no good to anyone. Berries are blanched, butter will not melt, fresh-baked bread has no smell.

It was hot and the sidewalks were shifting nervously. I lay on my bed with the window open and a washcloth over my eyes; it was the first day of a long weekend, and I was spending it with a migraine. Cass was driving up to the Russian River. Until the last minute I had meant to go with her, but by then I could scarcely move my eyes and I gave up. All the incomplete and damaged ventures of my life came to mind one after another. The poem cycle I would never finish. A friend in Boulder I was supposed to visit two years ago, and never called when I changed my plans. Learning to play the guitar. That girl I flirted with at Joanie's party, with the stupid name: Fury. I hid behind the natural sponges when she turned up at the store, but she saw me. That was the pattern: a moment of genuine interest, then a long, embarrassed retreat.

Finally I masturbated. Then I fell asleep with my fingers still stiffly crooked inside my underwear and my head thrust back into the pillow as if someone had just punched me in the face.

I woke up sweating, with the feeling I had just quit a dream of effortless energy, purpose, and interest—much more engaging than my real life. I kicked the covers off and fell back asleep. When I woke again I was damp and cold but my headache was better. It was raining.

My washcloth was a hot, wet mass under my right shoulder. I dug it out and scrubbed my face with it. My left eye was itching. In the bathroom, leaning into the mirror, the sink's edge cold against my stomach, I spread my eyelids to bare the eyeball and the lids' scarlet inpockets. I spotted the irritant, a red dot smaller than a pinhead, lodged under my lower lid near the tear duct.

I touched a twist of toilet paper to it, and the dot came away on the tip. I didn't know it was an egg. I thought it was something to do with my migraine—now that I had passed the object, the pain was gone. I was so grateful!

I dropped the twist in the toilet. If I had flushed, that would have been the end of the story, or at least of my part of it, but I did not. Some hours later, I hurried into the bathroom and peed without looking first. It was only when I stood and gave the bowl that respectful, melancholy look we give our rejectamenta that I saw the egg. It was the size of a Ping-Pong ball, and a shocking color against pee yellow.

I fished it out of the toilet with my hand, proof I was a little rattled, because I am usually fastidious. (I could have used salad tongs.) I washed the egg and my hands. The egg bobbled around my fingers. I felt no distaste or uneasiness. In fact, I felt an eager interest and relief. "It's an egg," I said out loud.

My first thought was that it was meant for Cass, not me. Cass would know what to do, she always did. She was at home being human. I was more like a bug in makeup: scratch the skin a little and you would uncover something black and chitinous, a bit of wing casing.

My second thought was quick and spiteful; it was that Cass must not find out. Deep down I thought that it was right for me to have the egg, not Cass; Cass didn't need it.

READING NOTES, JUNE 18

By some counts, hundreds, even thousands of humans have been swallowed by eggs. Many cases are poorly documented and we dare draw no conclusions from them. Some have acquired such a gloss of legend that it is difficult to sort out the fact from the fiction. But some are probably true. In a blizzard in the Himalayas in '59, three novice climbers and a Sherpa guide survived by creeping into an egg. In 1972, one-year-old Bobby Coddle crossed the Pacific in an egg, bobbing on the swells, and was pulled aboard a Japanese fishing boat, where he was extracted, in the pink of health, cooing with happiness.

I met Cass a long time ago, at college. It was the first week of freshman year, and our residential advisers had organized a square dance to help us all get acquainted. I was leaning on the fence watching and she came up and said, "I like you. You don't bother with this crap. You're like me." It wasn't true. I was wishing I weren't so uptight, that I could whirl around with the others, but I just smiled, feeling myself become the kind of person who stood aloof, instead of the kind who was always left out.

We became friends. I never knew why. I tried to please her, of course (everyone tried to please her), but I didn't expect to succeed: I was too stiff, too dour, and too uncertain. Cass was the kind of person who always knew what other people were saying about things, and whether they were right or wrong. And yet she changed her mind a lot, and never seemed to remember that she used to hold the exact opposite opinion. But knowing this didn't keep me from being ashamed when I got caught holding the wrong book, the wrong snack, the wrong shirt. "Do you *like* that?" she would say. Or, "You're not going to *wear* that, are you?" I would drop the object in question as if it had caught fire in my hands. I was ashamed of this, too; it was another thing Cass would not have approved of.

Cass discovered her lesbian tendencies after we graduated and immediately fell in love with the most beautiful girl I had ever seen, tall and stately, with long black hair and a fake ID (she was seventeen). I went out dancing with the two of them and got a migraine. Now Cass was seeing some guy with a goatee and I was the dyke, only I still hadn't met anyone who could pass the final test: make me forget Cass. I loved her, in a deep, unpleasant way, but I kept out of her bed. I survived her shifting passions by never becoming the object of them.

READING NOTES, JUNE 19

The folklore of eggs is flush with lucky breaks, but there are darker stories of lost children, vanished lovers, and besotted girls wasting away beside them. Two-time Iditarod champ Cath Summers set her dogs on a rival who boasted about possessing an egg, with fatal consequences (ironically, it turned out the rival was lying; the egg belonged to a neighbor, grocer Mary Over). In recent years, Professor Bev Egan, noted scholar of fascist architecture, starved to death during a vigil in the Santa Cruz mountains during which, she told friends, she expected an egg to appear to her.

I put the egg on a damp paper towel in the bottom of a mixing bowl and put the bowl under my bed, swathed in an old flannel shirt. By the time Cass came home the egg was as big as a baseball. I didn't show it to her.

It grew steadily. At one point I punched a small hole in it with a pencil and inserted a thermometer. The egg was almost body temperature. I would have liked to insert the thermometer into the very center, to see if the temperature was higher or lower there, but by then the egg was big enough that no ordinary thermometer would have reached so far. The hole I had made filled with fluid and shone like a tiny eye. The meat around it grew swollen; finally, it swelled enough to close over the hole. I tried other experiments: I swabbed a small area with rubbing alcohol—it seemed to contract; I rubbed salt on another spot—it shrank visibly and formed a shallow, wrinkled pit. I brushed it with oil—it glistened but did not otherwise alter; I spun it and it rotated as smoothly as a planet. I would have held a candle to it but that seemed barbarous. Nothing seemed to affect it much.

After a few days, the egg began to give off a sweetly fetid smell. I heard Cass stamping around in the kitchen when she got back from work. Then she banged on the door. "Where are all these *bugs* coming from? Do you have fruit in your room, Im?"

I said no. After a while she went away.

That night I took the egg to bed with me. It was about the size of a bowling ball. Since it was moist, I swathed it in a T-shirt and put a towel down under the bottom sheet. Then I curled around the egg and took comfort in its warmth against my stomach, though it was not a cold night.

In the middle of the night I awoke. My room seemed darker than usual. I realized that the egg had grown so big it blocked the light from the window. I could just make out its black curve against the ceiling. I was lying against it, almost under it, since as it grew it had overshadowed me. The shirt I had wrapped it in was in shreds around it. Maybe it was the sound of cloth tearing that had woken me. Fluid slowly spilled over my thighs and between them, and I thought with prim displeasure that I had wet myself in my sleep. But no. The egg had wet me.

I rolled from under it and spent the night on the sofa in the common room.

READING NOTES, JUNE 22

According to legend, the egg prevents canker sores and sudden falls, cures ringworm in horses, and kills mosquitoes. Whether or not these claims are true, the egg does bring undisputed benefits. Premature babies and patients recovering from surgery can often be coaxed to lick the egg for nourishment when they will take nothing else. Flesh wounds heal faster when bound against the egg, and in many hospital wards one may see patients in their white gowns splayed against the red orb in awkward attitudes, as if held there by gravity. They look like souls in the ecstasies of the last days; whether blessed or damned it is hard to say.

When I awoke on the couch, Cass was standing over me, arms folded. "What's going on, Imogen? You're not acting normal. Are you on drugs?"

I draped my blanket around me and shuffled toward my bedroom. Cass tried to pass me and I elbowed her back, but she got to my bedroom before me. She gasped out loud when she saw the egg.

Cass and I carried it down the stairs and into our tiny back patio in a blanket sling. We cleared a spot for it and I draped the blanket over it so no one would see it. I thought someone might try to steal it. I woke up three times that night to look out the window, but everything was quiet.

Cass came home the next day with a pile of books about eggs for me to read. I thought, *She's already trying to take over.* I thanked her.

"I might read them too," she said.

"I'll recommend one." I carried the whole pile into my room, shutting the door with my heel. I stuck them under the bed.

In the end I read them, of course. I studied them, even; I took notes. That was how Cass got her way, by being right.

READING NOTES, JUNE 26

You cannot make an egg from a lump of earth, and a haunch of beef carved into a sphere is also nothing like it, nor can one be fashioned from blood and barley, or suet and cinnebar, or indeed any substance whatever. I am confident that a trip to the moon would bring back no substance however new to earth that would in any kind resemble the egg.

Extraordinary as the egg already is, there are stories of an inner, more essential egg, a sort of distillate: a fragrant red crystal, which some propose as the "pill of immortality" described by Wei Po-Yang in the first half of the second century A.D.

I understood that the egg was mine to care for. I was to brood over it, the books agreed. What that meant was not quite clear. Was I supposed to sit on top of it? From the landing of the back steps I stretched one foot out to the top of the egg. My foot slipped and in catching my balance I banged my chin on the splintery rail. "What are you doing?" said Cass from above.

"Nothing," I said. It was almost a sob, but that was because my chin hurt. I sat down on the steps.

The books said that the egg would not grow to its full size without help. Without attention—love, yes, but also suspicion and fear, all of which push and pull inside the egg, awakening and differentiating it—it would be stunted, small and hard. They described this "abortion" in almost identical turns of phrase, as if reciting a lesson. "The neglected egg is dense and hard as a croquet ball. Flesh heaps on flesh in a rude aggregation, as a pearl forms in an oyster, or a tumor in place of a child." As if a bud opened on a wodge of fused petals. The egg would grow, somehow, without my care—eggs do. But what would it become? "A lay figure, stony, no better than a statue; a lifeless lump."

Reading Notes, June 29

"The eggs are obviously spacecraft. Some are reconnaissance vehicles. Some are mobile homes. You see little pinks and long reds. They peek out the windows. Or they descend, on beams of light. The pinks are the clever ones. The master race, if you will. They study us. They judge us. But the reds are there to intercede for us, to plead for mercy," said Cindy Halbschnitt, who was abducted and returned to tell her tale. "I wasn't afraid. I knew—how shall I put it?—I was loved."

I would brood, if that was what the egg needed. It was a worthwhile thing to do—maybe the only worthwhile thing to do, even if I didn't know why. And though it required an openness and sincerity that didn't come naturally, I thought that for the egg I could learn to love without reserve. Maybe the egg was my chance at what everyone else seemed to feel all the time: the cozy feeling of being-with, the worth-it-ness of love. But these thoughts were secondary. I would brood because I needed to. Being near the egg was like scratching *next to* an itch. The closer I got the more keenly I felt my separation from it.

My friends—Roky, Tim, Deedee—thought I'd make a joke out of it, remembering how I had smirked at Deedee's chanting circle, Tim's banana-tempeh power drinks. Cynical Imogen. In fact I had been waiting, hoarding myself, for that call.

Yes, it was a burden. That thought did cross my mind. There were other things in life: clever little shaggy ponies, surveillance devices, snowboarding. There were excellent curries. There was probably a girl reading Genet somewhere. She might like midcentury modern furniture, but she would come to understand my thrift store armchair, in time. But once the egg had come to me, it was impossible to imagine a life that didn't contain it.

READING NOTES, JULY 2

Some say we are trying to hatch Christ. Like Phanes, Eros, Nangarena: incubator babies all. Christ, Antichrist, Big Bird, God or Godzilla, who knows? We are undertaking a project itself entirely indefinite (yet with high, though vague standards), in anticipation of a result on which no one can agree. Why?

"Why?" said Roky. He turned the pegs on my dusty guitar, tuning it absentmindedly.

I could only answer that while the luster of adolescent fantasy might have dazzled me at first, it was the lusciousness and dignity of the egg itself that sealed my commitment to it. The egg was serious, even melancholy, but it knew how to play; it was quiescent, and yet teeming with life, rich with invention and innovation. It made no scenes and did not argue for itself, but answered all doubters by virtue of its unfeigned excellence.

"I don't know, I guess I'm curious," I said.

READING NOTES, JULY 3

Since we turn food into flesh our whole life long, the doctrine of bodily resurrection presents at least one problem. We form enough new cells in the course of living to reflesh ourselves many times over. Are some cells elected to immortality and others extinguished forever? The ingenious deity of the heretic sect that called themselves the Ovaries (before they were wiped out in 1265) provides for those extra cells, lumps them together and gives them a new life—as guides, as judges, as spies. As eggs. One might also call them angels.

I took the stuff from my Mrs. Potato Head kit down to the backyard and I punched two eyes, a nose, and a mouth into the egg. I kept them close together, a tiny face on the side of a planet. Juice from its puncture ran down the nose and hung off the tip.

"What are you?" I asked the face. There was silence, which I had expected. "Who are you? What is your name? I'll have it out of you in the end, old drippy head, your ghastly looks don't frighten me." But the egg said nothing. The summer was passing, the egg was growing, and I was no closer to knowing what to do with it. There seemed to be every chance of failing decisively, while success was a mystery of which none of the books ever spoke, except in the most general terms.

I leaned against the egg, and sank a little way into the pink wall. It was neither sticky nor slippery, just moist, like a healthy cheek on a warm day. I stroked the egg, then began palpating it rhythmically with my fists. I pressed my face against it until I needed air. I backed up, gasping. The egg was the most provocative thing I had ever seen. I was jealous of the flies that licked its crown, the ants that were already tasting its effluvium.

I sat down on a cinder block in the shade of the egg. My mouth was dry. The egg was full of water; each cell wall was healthily distended around a fat globule. I poked my finger into the egg and the hole slowly filled with clear fluid. I slid the tip of my tongue in the hole and lapped up the water. Then I sank my hand in and tore out a hunk. I chewed and swallowed until I had reduced the piece to a wad of gum, and then I rested, staring up at a seagull, until it disappeared behind the pink curve of the egg as if swallowed by it.

Reading Notes, July 6

The surface of the egg has been divided up into territories. Some cartographers of the egg—we might also call them phrenologists—name twelve principalities, others swear to twenty or thirty. Claims have been made for as many as ninety-nine.

Each principality is the purlieu of a given quality or affection. One is kindled by song, one by wit; one admires artifice, one multiplies complex fractions for sport. Numerological and astrological schemes are not neglected, and among all these, there is a bailiwick for you—yes, you. If you want the egg to take you in, you will need to knock at the right door.

I got up, intending to hurl myself headlong into the egg. But as always, something stopped me. Instead I took a paring of its flesh, the size and shape of a minnow. I carried it up to the kitchen, turned a burner on high, and jostled the scrap in a pan. It spat and flung itself about like something cooked alive—which perhaps it was—until I clapped a spatula on it and trapped it there, sizzling; then it was docile. But I burned my wrist on the edge of the pan trying to unstick the morsel, which I finally ripped off its own crisped skin. I folded it in a paper towel and sat in a corner, sniffing it, running it under my nose like a cigar, dropping it, almost on purpose, on my shirt, and peeling it up again from the greasy patch it left. Finally I stuck it in my mouth and chewed it up and ate it. It was linty.

The missing piece grew back. I was unchanged.

READING NOTES, JULY 8

The egg has many names: Terrestrial Moon, Lord of the Stones, the Invitation, Belly of the Ostrich, Excrement of the Moon, Animal Stone, God-pudding, Ore of Hermes; more jocularly, the Great Pumpkin, the Cheese Ball, or Humpty of Notre Dumpty; the Vegetable Meat, the Magnet, and the Blarney Stone.

The egg is manifold: called divine, it can be sliced thin and made into very passable sandwiches. The egg is magical and mundane, Baal and baloney. It's the all-purpose object of desire, the placeholder for every operation. My kingdom for an egg. Person, place, or egg. Egg, therefore I am.

I dreamed about a girl in a room. She was as white as paper and skinny. There was a hollow spike stuck in her side, attached to a rusty hand pump, and she worked the lever vigorously while blood splashed into a bucket. When the bucket was full, she pulled the spike out of her side, unhooked the bucket, and hurried with it to a sluice that fed through a tumbledown place in the wall. She dumped it in. Then she went back and started over. It seemed impossible that she have any blood left in her body, but more kept coming, thick and red. I was amazed she spent herself so unreservedly.

The day had been hot, multicolored and banging, full of groceries and loud with basketballs. Spilled smoothies turned to fruit leather on the sidewalk. The smells in alleys and stairwells grew unbearable.

The first bugs—winged ants or termites—went largely unnoticed, like most harbingers. One landed on my inventory book while I was writing. I brushed it off. One crawled industrously among my soaps, fell off, and continued its course on the floor. I had seen six or so before I looked outside and realized the air was full of them. On my break I joined a small crowd that was watching them come up out of a crack in the Wells Fargo parking lot. They dragged their wings clumsily through the openings like ladies in fancy dress forgetting the girth of their skirts. They came out of playgrounds, driveways, sidewalks. By dusk a cone of frenetic activity stood under each streetlight.

When I came home, it was dark. The room was cool blue, with a slight burnt smell of the city, of tarry roofs and exhaust. I went to close the window. The light wind of my movement blew frail things like snowflakes along the sill and off it. They fluttered down into the darkness.

I turned on the light. There were insects all over my bed. Some were alive and still pirouetting, dragging their stiff wings. Most were dead.

The egg was covered with them. Wing-thatched, it had turned white and opalescent. Some of the wings beat, others were still, pressed together like hands. The moon rose and the egg shimmered like a bride in a beautiful dress, and I made up my mind.

I took off my clothes and climbed in.

I say "climbed in." It was more strenuous than that. I lowered my head and ran at the egg, ramming my crown deep in the pulp. I got stuck there a moment, with my head caught, then slid my hands into the egg beside my ears, stretching the walls of the hole until I broke the vacuum seal. I felt the egg respond to the insult, fattening and stiffening around the cut, and in effect folding me in deeper, though perhaps the intent was to enclose me and keep me from doing any more damage. I pumped my hips and thrust my head and hands deeper, and though there was nothing to hold on to I managed to drive myself in farther, until I felt the egg close over my toes. Then I swam toward the center.

Intermission

(Two short films will be shown):

The Bad Egg
(Bolav Koule, 1982, Dir. Hubert Slameňého, Czechoslovakia, 13 min., color, 35mm: live action plus stop-motion animation; subtitled)

The sagging drapes are imperfectly drawn together against the heavy yellow sun, which leans on the south wall like a drunk. The faded purple velvet fills the room with a pungent, even hysterical fuchsia light. The flunky who hurries around, heavy silver salver slithering in his sweating hands, fears and hates the room. On a soaked and blackened Persian carpet rests the room's mistress: an ancient egg, so large the lowest pendants of the chandelier lie about its crown like a tiara.

The egg does not look healthy, physically or morally. From age and dissipation, the pink flesh has hardened and blackened, as if scorched by a terrible fire. Her skin is a mosaic of scabs, and from the cracks leaks a thin, blood-streaked pus. Flies hang conspicuously around, beading on the stained curtains, then rising all together as if jerked up on stiff wires and swished around (and in fact you can see the wires if you look for them).

The filmmakers have contrived to make the egg utterly loathsome, yet seductive in a tawdry way, like an old whore. She wears a stained lace apron the size of a hankie, which serves to render her substantial nakedness obscene. She is both foul and decorative, a rotten tomato oozing onto a doily.

The egg sings a snatch of song in a slurred voice, weeping crocodile tears from every crack. The flunky flutters around, wiping away the tears with innumerable tissues he pulls one at a time out of a box in quick succession, like a stage routine. The tissues stick to the egg; when they are pulled off bits stay behind.

An alarm clock rings: the flunky swishes officiously over to a little marble table and returns with a hypodermic, which he plunges between two scabs. The egg shudders, then hollows her side walls as a person might hollow her cheeks, and sucks the needle dry.

She shimmies, then settles herself. The flies come to rest on her hide.

As she relaxes, the cracks flare; mucous membrane bulges in the gaps. Her slip is showing.

But what's this? A pecking at the window, a peeking and a

peeping? An innocent little child! Or rather, a child not quite so innocent as she should have been, a bold child who looks through windows, a peeping tomboy who is fascinated by what is rank and sour and self-involved. Not a frank and open child, but a complicated and curious one.

But see, the egg has noticed the child. Her hide ripples, the flies flash blue and green, she draws herself in so the sides of her cracks crimp together. "Let her in," drawls the egg, and the flunky opens the window.

The child throws one leg over the sill, and hesitates. "Come in," purrs the egg. Then sharply: "Come in!" The cracks flare all over; it is like a flamenco dancer's flash of red petticoats. The egg pulls herself up, her fissures spread like wings, or gills, or the frills of a peculiar mushroom. The mucous insides pulse and fizz. Spritz. A heavy yellow vapor stands in a cloud around the egg for a suspended moment, and then wends its way, lazily, toward the open window. It looks like a feather boa come to life, and it wraps itself cozily around the little girl's neck.

She coughs, sags on the sill, then slips dreamily over and stands before the egg. How can a sphere move like a cobra? The egg dances in front of the girl. "Grease me, little girl. Make my skin feel nice," croons the egg, and a crockery pot appears suddenly at her base, as if she has been roosting on it. "Butter your egg," says the egg. "Stroke it on, nice and thick."

The little girl scoops out a handful of fat and stands holding it uncertainly, then pats it against the leathery wall.

"Not like that, dear. Stroke it in. Find the dry places with your clever little fingers."

It is tricky work; there are many scaly bits to press the ointment under and around, so she gets very absorbed; and when she draws near one of the cracks she hardly notices, though the great mass sways toward her, like a horse guiding the curry-comb toward an itchy spot, and only when her fingers slide right around the edge of the crust to the slippery interior does she pause.

"Ohhh!" neighs the egg. "Don't stop! Deeper!" So the girl gets a new blob of fat and begins stroking it on the lubricious reds and pinks, which hardly seem to need it. The walls suck her hands. "Oh, the relief you give me! Deeper, child, deeper!" The child puts one little shoe up on the edge of the rift, and leans forward. She is in up to her shoulder. The egg screams, "NOW!" The girl reaches back with her other toe for the floor, but it is too late; the flunky has rushed forward, and now thrusts the little girl deep into the egg, until she quite disappears. The egg goes very still.

After a minute the egg shifts uneasily, burps, and lays two little shoes in a puddle on the floor.

The Good Egg
(Le Bon Oeuf, 1951, Dir. Hervé Blanc, France, 11 min., color, 35mm)

The camera is gliding through an orchard. Large, improbably neat and identical leaves part and slide away soundlessly to either side. We pass through secret green spaces. A chartreuse inchworm is disclosed. It quests in the air, then claps its end to a knobbly twig. We clear a crooked branch. We round a mossy trunk, pass a tidy nest overstuffed with fluffy fledglings. Leaves again, held up like cards for a magic trick, then smoothly removed, one, two, three, to reveal a hill, green, carefully dotted with daisies.

Daffodils wag unnaturally in the motionless grass. Ducks show off their majolica beaks. The little girl near the top of the hill carries a bucket and her fat yellow braids whack her cheeks. A zephyr ruffles her bangs. She looks up.

Lo! The good egg. It descends from a baby blue sky to the sound of wind chimes. The maid drops her bucket and clasps her hands together. The screen goes white. Out of the whiteness, like a reflection in milk, a figure emerges. It's the maid, but her hair is unbound, her form newly slender. Her transfigured features fill the screen.

The egg hovers above her like a round pink blimp. Jill rises to her toes, stretching her fingers toward the egg. The egg wobbles amusingly and descends a little farther. The tops of the daffodils tickle its underbelly and it jiggles all over with mirth.

Jill rights the bucket and sets it under the egg. Then she leans her face against the side of the egg. The visual rhyme of rosy cheek and cheek is established in a close-up. She begins to palpate the side of the egg with her round fists. Left, right, left, right, push, push, push, go the insistent little fists. Jill's eyes are dreamy. Birds twirl around the rapt couple.

Quite suddenly, from somewhere underneath the egg (the camera demurs) comes the flow. What looks like pink lemonade splashes, sparkling, into the wooden bucket. Jill's fists pump the side of the egg. The squirts strengthen, whipping the juice into a froth.

When the bucket is full, Jill plunges both hands into it. She slurps greedily from her hands. Then she sets the bucket on a rock.

She stands. The sky shows through the egg's suddenly diaphanous sides. Jill's hands hang at her sides. Slowly, with measured steps, she approaches the egg. The pink veils part, and she steps inside. We see her turn and seat herself; then the veils are drawn again and the egg lifts into the air. It is drawn away on the wind. Tiny clouds throng around it.

On the hilltop below, a small boy (the tardy Jack) discovers the bucket. The field is suddenly full of village folk, dressed in white. They are tilting their heads back and waving to Jill as she disappears. Then they gather around the bucket.

Oddly, the ending is much the same as that of *The Bad Egg*.

Part Two

In the center of the egg, immobilized by the clasp of its flesh, I felt incredibly calm.

But how hard I was, how gnarled and dense, like the pit of a peach. The sweet flesh was wet and clung all around me, but I was caught in a furious refusal, despite all my longing. Beauty was all around me (The splendid surplus! A blazing chrysanthemum!) but I stuck to myself like a scab.

It is the nature of a thing to be inert; oh how our alchemists must coax and wheedle the thing to kindle spirit in it, and then whoosh goes the vapor out the chimney, leaving behind a bit of treacle in a jar. We study to be things, impressed by their steadfastness. Why, you can swallow a stone, and find it in the toilet bowl in the morning, unchanged; we dream of such obduracy. But that is not our nature, we are built to slump, trickle, and run; waters sluice through us, and we are curious and fond. Bruised as a child (but no more than most people), I had learned to sit in shit like a stone and smell nothing and betray nothing. I had supposed that there was some reward—the curtailment of pain, at least. Now I know the reward: to become that stone.

Dear egg, melt me! I have practiced permanence, yes, but only to keep myself for you. I would drop my bones in an instant to leap to your mouth in one soft, elated blob. I could be yolk, albumen, and water; I could be the most delicate syllabub, scented with rose water and cardamom. I am Turkish delight, I am marzipan, taste me, take me!

When I emerged from the egg, disgusted and humiliated, dripping a pink syrup that now seemed filthy to me, I was not congratulated or bumped on the bottom. Nothing had happened. The burn on my wrist had healed and my complexion would stay clear for two weeks afterwards, but I had not gone in for a spa treatment.

There were my clothes, flung about with an abandon I now thought was ridiculous. I sat on the ground and wiped myself with my wadded socks. Then I put my clothes back on. I thought I had never done anything so terrible.

I packed a bag and went to Boulder to visit my friend. She was pleased to see me, slightly less pleased when she realized I had no particular plans to leave. After a while I began to do some of the things I used to do: watch movies, read, write a little. I didn't call the store or Cass. I kept checking myself, to see if I was changed. Perhaps I had misunderstood, and the egg's rejection of me was itself a rite of passage I had not recognized, because I had my own idea of what translation should feel like. But there was nothing different about me except for this checking itself—the flinching and squinting and double takes in the mirror.

Maybe disappointment was enlightenment, and this acquaintance with futility was the closest I would come to God.

READING NOTES, JULY 14

In cabalistic tradition, the number *one* is not an abstraction, but the proper name of the egg. We do not count *one*—any child knows you don't need an abacus to see how many one is—we say its name. Egg, two, three. This is not to say that *two* means two eggs. The egg is singular and sufficient. It is not a unit or a building block.

I came back to San Francisco on a windy, blond day: cotton shirts, flags, dog walkers in shorts and mustaches. An old man stooped to pick up a hose as I walked past his yard. He had thinning yellow hair, and the rim of his ear was soft and red. He had a huge boil on the side of his neck by the collar of his turquoise shirt; it was so swollen it was almost spherical, and the wrinkled skin stretched over it until it was as tight and shiny as a child's.

I passed the playground, where a few kids were working in the sandbox with bright blue plastic buckets and spades. A little girl looked up at me: a little girl with no face. A smooth pink globe seemed to supplant her head. Then the bubble collapsed and she sucked it back into her mouth.

I walked right past my house. I wasn't quite ready.

In the coffee shop, I noticed the chipmunk cheeks of the girl working there, and her breasts, which strained the vintage print she was wearing, and her upper arms—she had cut off the sleeves of the dress—which swung vigorously as she frotted the steamer wand with a yellow towel. She had the thin white scars of a decorative cutting on her shoulder—a rough circle. Everyone is made of spheres, and the world is round.

READING NOTES, JULY 15

The egg might more properly be seen as the ambiguous zero, which sits at the center of the number line, but is scarcely a number itself. The List of Lists does not include itself, you will not find the Book of Books in its own bibliography, the King of Kings does not kowtow to the crown. When all matter is totted up, one thing remains: the egg itself.

Cass opened the door. "Imogen," she said.

I went straight through the apartment and out the back. She followed me. "Things are a little different around here, if you're interested," she said. But the egg still lay in the tiny backyard, even bigger than before, wedged half under the shed roof, with the clothesline cutting through it like a cheese wire. It seemed the worse for wear, and there was pink oil all over the concrete near it. Three large, nearly bald cats were lapping at the puddle. They scattered over the fences when the door banged, kicking up their bare bottoms like impossibly nimble babies.

A moment later I saw what I thought was a hurt mouse humping along the base of the fence and disappearing down a hole; after a moment I understood that what I had seen was a featherless bird, using its stubby, plucked wings like crutches.

"They come into the kitchen," said Cass. "They've actually scared away the rats. And check this out." She stepped over to our failed vegetable garden. A pink mound like an exposed turnip broke the surface. She drummed her fingers on it and it contracted. Then a fleshy end as big as a woman's heel poked up through the dirt. "The neighbors complained, but it's perfectly harmless." She drew it gently out of the ground. "It's huge," she said. The worm butted against her wrists like a blind puppy.

Cass was panting shallowly. Her cheeks were red and shiny and distended, her eyelids fat. Her eyebrows had gone pale, or maybe even fallen out. She had drawn in thin, brown, artful brows, but these, not perfectly symmetrical, did not work with her cartoon farmwife cheeks, her cherry lips.

"What's going on, Cass?" I said.

"What do you mean?"

"You look strange. I think you've been eating my egg."

"*Your* egg!"

"I grew it. It grew on me," I said.

"You walked out on it. And on me. I had no idea where you were. Just because—" She paused. I thought she might not say it, but she did. "Just because it didn't want you!"

I threw myself on her. The worm writhed violently between us, then escaped. We struggled on the ground in the syrup. The Mexican guys in the apartment across from us came out on their landing, laughing and hooting. *"Putas! Marimachas!"*

Late that night I woke up and looked out the window. The fog was purple and mauve, saturated with city light. Across the way a light was on in an empty kitchen. Down in the yard I could see Cass leaning against the egg. She was licking it.

I dreamed Cass grew fat, shiny, red. As she waxed, the egg waned. At last she was almost spherical, a powerful figure, staring like an idol. The egg was the size of a malt ball, and she picked it up and popped it in her mouth. Then she turned toward me and opened her arms. Her sparse hair streamed from the pink dome of her skull, her eyes rolled, her teeth struck sparks off one another, and her hands were steaks, dripping blood. Now I knew her. She was the egg. I turned to run, but her arms folded around me, and I sank back into her softness, and awoke pinioned by my comforter, on the side of the bed.

READING NOTES, JULY 19

Ancient Persian mystics write that the universe is an oyster. Our incessant desires and demands annoy it; we are the itch in the oyster. Around our complaints a body forms. The egg begins as a seed pearl. It grows beautiful. For this treasure, princes would pauper themselves. To harvest the pearl, we would pry the earth from the sky, though the satisfaction of our desires would destroy the universe and us with it. But be warned. The egg is the gift that robs you, for its germ is pure need: gain it and you will lack everything.

After breakfast the next morning I went down and unlocked the gate across the alley between our house and the neighbors'. There was a heap of splintery boards blocking the alley. I carried them back a few at a time and piled them in the yard. On the other side of the fence, the neighbor's dog went up and down the alley with me, whining softly. When the way was clear I went back to the egg.

I rocked it back and stuck a board under it, and then I squeezed behind it and rocked it forward onto the board, and stuck another under it behind. Then I rocked it back and fit another board onto the first. In this way I raised it little by little. It took me several hours to raise the sagging center a few feet off the ground. That was far enough. I got down on my stom-

ach. Syrup hung in sticky cords between the bottom of the egg
and the pavement. They snapped across my face as I squirmed
beneath the egg. Once the egg's center of gravity was directly
above me I gathered my legs under me. The egg gave slightly
above me, allowing me to crouch. The boards creaked, but
held.

I stretched my arms out to either side.

Somehow, I stood up.

I took a step. I was carrying it.

There was a thump and scrabble behind me and I started.
The egg pitched to one side, but I took a quick step and righted
it. The red face of a huge cat was staring from the top of the
back fence. Then it jumped down into the yard and padded toward me. I turned back toward the alley. Two more cats
crouched menacingly in my path, but as I staggered toward
them, they slunk to either side, and then turned in after me.

Little by little I made my way down the alley toward the
street. The dog kept hurling itself against the fence beside me.
Syrup ran down my face and body and drizzled on the sidewalk. My footsteps sounded like kisses.

"Imogen!"

I turned carefully.

Cass was standing at the top of the front steps in her dressing
gown. "Wait, Imogen! Please!" She whirled; I saw the pink
flash of her heel as she dashed up the apartment stairs.

I continued on my way. The dog finally crashed through the
fence and came bounding up. Six cats slunk after him, followed
by a corps of creeping birds. I turned left down Eighteenth
Street. I crossed Church. Guerrero. Valencia. People made way.
Someone dropped a burrito and it burst, black beans rolling
across the sidewalk in front of me. We walked across them.

Someone pushing a shopping cart fell in behind me; I could hear the wheels rattling.

When the light changed at Mission I stopped too suddenly. The egg bounced through the traffic and fetched up in the doorway of a doughnut shop. The whores that hung out there gathered around it, touching it, then tasting their fingers. Cass caught up with me and when the light changed we walked across the street together.

The egg was torn. Things were stuck to it: pebbles, bottle caps, lottery stubs, a blue condom, an empty popper, a parking ticket. I brushed it off. The whores helped, dabbing it with napkins from the doughnut shop. The animals milled around our feet.

Cass waited. I saw she had the worm slung around her neck.

I crouched down with my back to the egg while it was trapped in the doorway and tried to stand up, forcing it up the wall. When they saw what I was doing, two guys came forward and lifted it for me. I started off down the street at what was almost a jog, heading south now, out of the city. My strange train bounced, slunk, hobbled after. Some of the whores came too. The shopping-cart man was there. Two kids carrying a huge boom box between them joined us.

Cass fell in behind.

SPERM

Nobody can remember when the sperm became large enough to see, but we agree on this: once that point was reached, every generation topped the last. They went from guppy to goldfish, and before long they could frighten a schnauzer, and not much later even Great Danes made way for them. And while it looks like at buffalo-heft they've stopped growing, it's possible they're just gathering their resources for another leap. We are afraid that the sperm will grow as big as rhinoceroses and hunt us down, but we are much more afraid that they will again grow tiny, that we will have to go back to the screens and meshes we remember from our grandmothers' doors. What if they grow so small filters will not stop them? How will we protect ourselves?

Sperm are ancient creatures, single-minded as coelacanths. They are drawn to the sun, the moon, and dots and disks of all descriptions, including periods, stop signs, and stars. They worship at nail heads, doorknobs and tennis balls. More than one life has been saved by a penny tossed in the air.

· · ·

The sperm cabaret is coming to town, and Virginia and I are going to see them. The trained sperm are squeezed into specially made costumes, and they dance and flop about, she says, very comically! Can you picture a sperm in a little hat held on with suction cups (an ingenious device explained in the program)? And sporting a very large cravat-cum-cummerbund? They even utter some sort of sound, which I cannot imagine would be very musical, but Virginia says that although guttural, the cry of the spermatozoa is weirdly haunting, and the au courant are scrambling to acquire recordings.

It is hard to believe that the great marble fountains of Brussels, which depict young spermatozoa disporting themselves in the spray, were once considered masterpieces. Few any longer take the time to decipher the complex symbolism that informs these mammoth atrocities. One wonders how a pest as common as pigeons could ever have been elevated, even in metaphor, to the status of gods. From time to time citizens' groups petition for the demolition of the eyesores, but there is always some sentimentalist or self-appointed keeper of tradition who rallies the public around the monuments, which do at least provide the children of Brussels welcome places to play in hot weather.

The Sperm Conservation Corps is lobbying to reserve a portion of the sperm's natural habitat as a protected zone, off limits to sportswomen and the food industry. Opponents, from logging concerns to public safety watchdogs, point out that the natural habitat of pest and parasite is much too close to home, and that there is at any rate no shortage of sperm. Passenger pigeons once darkened the sky, the lobbyists reply; imagine a world without sperm!

. . .

Surely we have all gone for a stroll in a bucolic landscape, sperm far from our minds, and rounded a curve to see a sleek black ovoid crouched menacingly athwart the path. Though ordinarily timid, sperm have a bullish persistence when their tiny minds are fixed on one object. In some cases the old wives' trick will work: rap them sharply on the "nose" with whatever comes to hand. The sting will startle and confuse them, and they may simply amble away. If they do, count yourself lucky, and clear out. If they give chase, remember your lucky penny!

When you see a sperm whose coat looks "sueded" or has a greenish tint, it is an old boar and probably cunning. Play your cards well. If you make a kill, though, you are in for a treat. The meat of these dotards is gamy, and must be marinated for twenty-four hours at least before it is tender enough to chew (weigh it down with a stone or it will rise to the surface of your marinade—sperm do float!—and your hours of waiting will be for naught), but many gourmets consider their flavor more sophisticated than the popular meat of pup sperm, something like a fine aged cheese.

To clean a young sperm, first seize it by the base of the tail. Be careful: they are extremely muscular and will attempt to free themselves. It takes a strong stomach not to flinch when a slippery tail twines around your wrist, but persevere; one solid whack on the edge of a table should stun the creature. Then you must core it to remove the brain. An apple corer will do if the sperm is small; for larger sperm a professional's tool is essential. Aim well; it is possible to miss the brain altogether, since it is very small. Jam the blade into the back of the sperm, near the tail. It is best to drive the corer deep into the sperm with one blow, penetrating the thick blubber, which otherwise will wobble and suck at the blade, spoiling your aim. Once the firmer meat is reached, it is a simple matter to drive the blade deeper, turning it the while. When the blade breaks through the opposite side, push the solid handle through, ejecting the pith. Examine the cylinder for the pale blue of the brain. All remnants of brain matter must be removed or the recipe will be ruined; the brain will regenerate and the cooked sperm will begin to twitch. If the sperm has been chopped or pureed this effect will be all the more disturbing. (If swallowed induce vomiting.)

My favorite recipe is this: lay the sperm directly on the burner. As the skin crackles and splits, releasing the liquors, turn the sperm. When it is entirely relaxed, remove and cool. Peel off the bitter skin with a fork, and discard. Under it you will find a layer of translucent fat. Cut this off, press it through clean muslin and reduce it to the consistency of gruel over a low flame. Run the skinned sperm under a broiler to brown, garnish with orange slices, and top with the reduced liquors.

With a little ingenuity, the sperm's incredible propulsive power can be harnessed for your own enjoyment! Not just for professional daredevils, this sport can be enjoyed by practically anyone with a sense of adventure—and a few friends ready to lend a hand. Lure the sperm into a large net bag (used bags can be acquired cheap from many sporting goods stores). Cinch the bag tight around the sperm's tail. Secure your boat to the bag with a few sturdy ropes and launch it. Whee! Carry a stick: a poke at the right moment will help steer the beast. But not to worry: the sperm's own self-protective instincts will keep you clear of most obstacles.

I trap them in nets I string up across their trails and sell them to a guy down in L.A. who puts them on TV. You know, those shows where they got to rassle the gladiators in the ring. Everyone knows the shows are rigged anyway, they dope the sperm, so I don't know why they bother to get the dangerous ones, I guess they want them big. Of course sometimes they guess wrong on the dosage or they get a real sly one or something and he lays the chick out just like that! Gladiator my ass, they're just models, gals who couldn't make it on the runway or old ones on the way down. You know who's the real gladiator? Take a wild fucking guess!

Yes, they're cute! You may be tempted to try to keep young sperm as pets, and it's true that hatchlings will remain small almost indefinitely, if kept in a small bowl or terrarium. But you must not forget that these so-called bonsai sperm are not the bumbling infants they resemble. They are cunning and they hold a grudge. It is neither humane nor prudent to keep them from answering "the call of the wild."

At times, for reasons we don't fully understand, the normally evasive spermatozoon will form a permanent bond with one woman. When the sperm is young, the woman may be inclined to subtly encourage this fidelity, perhaps without even knowing she is doing so. As the sperm grows older and some awareness penetrates its puny brain of the gulf that separates it from the beloved, the relationship turns treacherous. The sperm will stalk her with increasing cunning. Sperm can bounce several stories, and their elasticity also enables them to squeeze through improbably small spaces. In the movie theater where she has sought refuge, she will spot the ominous dome across the aisle, dully reflecting the changing light. In the ladies' room she will see a glistening tail on the floor of the next stall. Outside the window of the restaurant where she is holding hands with her date something will rise and fall in the dark, blotting out the city lights below. The clever antics of a pup are not so cute when the sperm is fully grown. Indeed, the mature sperm are all the deadlier for their devotion, and more than one woman has been crushed to death by a creature she once jounced on her lap.

Sperm-brain swallowing is considered dangerous by the medical establishment, but devotees disagree. What is known is that the sperm brain does not die all at once but forms a temporary bond with the stomach lining, marshaling an unknown number of the host's cells to its service for as long as six hours, after which time the brain is digested and the host cells revert to their usual condition. Doctors claim the "high" users report is largely imaginary, but stories are consistent of a spreading "spermishness": a sense of haste and unstoppable purpose. The concomitant disregard for personal injury, property, or propriety can lead swallowers to extravagant ventures, some criminal or self-destructive, some visionary. Great works of art have been inspired by sperm-brain swallowing; so have hideous crimes, including the infamous "Ballet of Decapitations."

The cloud image of a sperm stretched out across the sky over Lisbon and again in Nubia has been taken for a sign by cultists who await the day they will be "exalted" into the creatures they worship, and allowed to join their packs. Adherents are gathering in public places, where they drop to their stomachs en masse and undulate in imitation of the movements of their totem. Ironically, several of these "Spermists" have fallen prey to bona fide members of the species who do not seem to recognize their special status.

We lodge our sperm in stalls we have painted with polka dots, and curry them with soft brushes and chamois cloths. We show them the spigot so that they may approve it, then tamp the sharp end into their side with a small mallet, and hook on the bucket. The milk is thick and sweet. Fresh, it is an aphrodisiac. It is also good for the digestion and, rubbed on the face, it clears the complexion. Reduced and dried in cakes it makes a nutritious trail bar and a good soap. We are working on a motor that will run on sperm milk. We do make good money from our products, but we channel it all back into the sacred community, to buy softer bedding for our sperm, and hire musicians to play the songs they love.

Once numerous, their herds raised a line of dust across the Great Plains, racing the locomotive. This opening sequence has become a cliché of film westerns: dust first, then a line of bobbing backs stretching across the screen. The nearby whistle of the train; some of the sperm cross the tracks, some turn, some scatter. Beside the tracks as the train thunders by, a sperm slumps in the dirt, transfixed by an arrow. Its oily coat is covered with dust, dung, and straw. It looks like a breaded drumstick.

. . .

The midwestern strain of the spermatozoa, who ravage wheat fields in bouncing armies, is lighter in color and has unusual markings which help to conceal it in tall grass. While most sperm drop their tiny young in water, these have devised other means of providing their offspring the moist environment they need. In early summer, the adults congregate head to head in small circles of five to eight and begin to blow wetly through their snouts. They puff and bubble until they work up a sizable mound of viscous foam, then position themselves and insert the infant sperm deep within the trembling dome. The outside of the dome soon hardens to a glassy sheen under the sun and prevents further drying. The dim shadows of the young can be seen to pike and writhe from time to time, but the hug of the thick foam holds them safely in suspension. They grow all summer long undisturbed—their only real enemy, aside from the occasional vigilant farmer with a pickaxe, is a species of heron that has adapted its long bill for the purpose of drilling through the dome and spearing the baby sperm. However, since the bird rarely catches more than one sperm at a time through the small hole it has gone to such pains to open, it poses little threat to the sperm population as a whole. By fall the spermatozoa are large and restless, and their dark skins are clearly visible through the dome. Here we see nature's genius: the shells that withstood sun and wind so imperviously melt in minutes under the first warm rain. The sperm are released into the wet grass. They lie there, quivering with surprise. Then they take their first timorous bounce.

FOETUS

The first fœtus was sighted in the abandoned hangar outside our town. Just floating there, almost weightless, it drifted down until its coiled spine rested on the concrete and then sprang up again with a flex of that powerful part. Then the slow descent began afresh. It was not hiding. It was not doing anything, except possibly looking, if it could see anything from between its slitted lids. What was it looking at? Possibly the motes of dust, as they drifted through the isolated rays of sun and changed direction all at once like birds flying together. Or at the runic marks of rust and bird shit on the walls. Maybe it was trying to understand them, though that might be imposing too much human order on the fœtus, who is known, now, for being interested in things *for* (as they say) *their own sake*—incomprehensible motive to most of us!

The fœtus rarely opens its eyes when anyone is watching, but we know they are deep blue-black, like a night sky when space shows through it, and its gaze is solemn, tender, yet so grand as to be almost murderous.

. . .

"We weren't afraid," said little Brent Hadly, who with his cousin Gene Hadly made the discovery, and took the first photos—we've all seen them—with his little point-and-shoot. "We thought it was Mr. Fisher in one of his costumes." (Mr. Fisher is one of those small-town loonies affectionately tolerated by the locals. He did indeed don a fœtus costume, later on, and paraded down to the Handimart parking lot—where he gulled some big-city newsmen, to their chagrin.) "Then my daddy came and said, 'Cut the fooling, Fisher!' " But even when the Fisher hypothesis had been disproved, no one felt anything but gentle curiosity about the visitor. Indeed, they scarcely noticed it had drifted near the small crowd while they debated, and trailed after them when they left.

The fœtus is preternaturally strong. It grabs its aides and knocks their bald heads together. It carries pregnant women across busy streets. It helps with the groceries. These are the little ways it enters the daily life of its parishioners: it turns over the soil in an old woman's garden. It lifts waitresses on tables to show off their legs. The fœtus has a formal appreciation for old-fashioned chivalry, and expects to be thanked for such gestures.

The fœtus roved about the town until it found a resting place to its liking in the playground of the municipal park, among dogs and babies. The mothers and the professional loiterers appointed themselves guards and watched it sternly, heading off the youngsters who veered too near it, but they softened to it over time, began to bring sandwiches and lemonade along and make casual speculations about the fœtus's life span, hopes, and origins. When the crowds of tourists pressed too close, they became the fœtus's protectors, and formed a human chain to keep them out.

Nobody's enemy and nobody's friend, it hides its heart in a locked box, a secret stash, maybe a hollow tree in the woods under a bees' nest, maybe a tower room on a glass mountain on a wolf-run isle in a sea ringed by volcanoes and desert wastes. The fœtus always keeps its balance.

Someone observed that the land seemed disarranged. Bent treetops, flattened grass, weeds dragged out of their seats, clods dislodged. Tedious speculations about crop circles and barrows and Andean landing strips made the rounds. Of course, we knew the fœtus's little feet dragged when he walked. We had seen the marks in the sandbox at the park. We should have noticed the resemblance, but we resisted the idea that the fœtus was only a transient resident. We had grown accustomed to, even proud of it; the fœtus was a municipal landmark. It had put our town on the map and filled it with visitors, so that our children had a chance to envy the latest haircuts, and our adults the latest cars and sexual arrangements.

Plus, the marks were disturbing. They were careless. They passed over (sometimes through) fences, even when the gate swung close at hand. Mrs. Sender's oleanders were uprooted and dragged for miles. Even after we knew the fœtus caused the marks, a mystery clung to them. For everything the fœtus did, though, there was someone to praise it. Followers did their following on the paths it left. They said the paths proposed an aesthetic that could not at once be grasped. Some began dragging a foot behind them as they walked, scorning markless movement as noncommittal, therefore cowardly. But why was the fœtus so restless? Was it seeking something? We had all seen it peering through our curtains in the evening, and found the marks in our flowerbeds in the morning. Was it exercising, or aimlessly wandering? Or was it writing a kind of message on the earth? Was it driven from rest by some torment, a plague personal to it, or a plaguey thought it couldn't shake: was the fœtus guilty?

Since the fœtus arrived, none of us has loved without regret, fucked without apprehension, yearned without doubt. We break out in a rash when a loved one comes near because we know the fœtus is there too, waiting for us to prove to it everything it already knows.

Was the fœtus a fœtus? Indeed it resembled one. But if it was, the question had to be raised: when the fœtus grew up, as it must, what would it become? Perhaps we all breathed a sigh of relief when scientists concluded that the fœtus, like the famous axolotl, was a creature permanently immature. Hence its enormous susceptibility, its patience and its eagerness to please. Like the unicorn, it adored virgins, but it had a raging fascination with sexual doings, a fascination that drove April Tip and the rest of her gang, the bad girls and boys of our town, to cruel displays under the streetlights around the park.

At first, though not for long, we believed our fœtus was unique. Of course we speculated about the home it must have had somewhere else, about *others*. But here on earth it seemed a prodigy, *the* prodigy. Soon enough, however, more of them began to appear. Some dropped out of the sky, people said, slowly and beautifully, their light heads buoying them up. Commentators waxed eloquent and bade us imagine, on the blue, a dot that grew to a pink dot that grew to a kewpie doll that became the creature we know now. Many were found, like the first one, swaying gently in some warm and secret enclosure—warehouses, high school gyms, YMCA dressing rooms. Publicity seekers claimed to have come across foetuses in infancy: tiny, playful, and virtually blind, like kittens, they bumbled around, falling on their oversized heads, and eagerly sucked on a baby finger, or indeed anything of like size and shape. One was reportedly discovered in a bird's nest, opening its tiny translucent lips among the beaks. But foetuses this small have never been held in captivity, or even captured on film. Whether that is because the susceptible creatures lose themselves in their surroundings, striving to become air, a patch of dirt, a falling leaf, or because they never existed in the first place, hardly matters, for the situation remains that none are found, except in stories that are already far from firsthand by the time they reach a credible authority. But we may pause for a minute to wonder whether, if such kittens do exist, they are the offspring of our original foetus, who for all we know may be capable of fertilizing itself, like some plants, or if they grow from spores that have drifted here from some impersonally maternal comet, or—most mysterious thought of all—whether they spring up in our world self-generated, as sometimes new diseases appear to do, teaching us new pains, just because the world has left a place open for them.

Behind one another's eyes, it is the foetus we love, floating in the pupil like a speck, like a spy. It's looking over your shoulder, making cold drinks even colder, and it doesn't care what promises you've made. We think we want affection, sympathy, fellow feeling, but it is the cold and absolute we love, and when we misplace that in one another we struggle for breath. Through the pupil's little peephole, we look for it: the shapeless, the inhuman.

Of course, with such a company of admirers, sycophants, interpreters, opportunists, advisers, prophets, and the like behind it, it wasn't long before the fœtus was performing many of the offices once seen to by our local pastor: visiting the sick, hosting charitable functions, giving succor to troubled souls. One day Pastor Green simply left town, and no one was very sorry. It was the graceful thing to do, people agreed, and saw to it that the fœtus stood behind the pulpit the next Sunday. At first it held an honorary post; we couldn't settle on a suitable title, but we did present it with a robe and a stiff white collar, which it seemed to admire. Higher-ups in church office were rumored to be uneasy about this unorthodox appointment, but public feeling was behind it. And there was no question that the fœtus would increase the church's subscription thousandfold; no one had ever seen such a benefit potluck as the first one hosted by the fœtus. It wielded the ice cream scoop with tireless arm and paid personal attention to every dessert plate.

Of course, the fœtus preferred to hold services in the sandbox, and the citizens appreciated this gesture as a call to simplicity and a sign of solidarity with regular folk. How the fœtus managed to lead us may be hard to understand. At first, its role was to inspire and chide. But it soon felt its way into the post, and began performing those gestures that mean so much to our town: choosing the new paint color for the courthouse (the fœtus preferred mauve), pouring the first bucket of cement for the new tennis courts. (We could afford it, for money was rolling in: tourists, visiting scholars, and zealots continued to come, prepared to shop, and after a short bewilderment we provided all the kiosks, booths, and lemonade stands they required.) Our fœtus made the covers of the major newsmagazines, and meanwhile, the copycat fœtuses were turning up everywhere, and the rich were installing them in their homes.

The fœtus is made of something like our flesh, but not the same, it is a sort of *über* flesh, rife with potentialities (for the fœtus is, of course, incomplete—always; unfinished—perpetually), it is malleable beyond our understanding, hence unutterably tender, yet also resilient. A touch will bruise the fœtus, the nap of flannel leaves a print on its skin. The fœtus learns from what it neighbors, and may become what it too closely neighbors. Then your fœtus may cease to be; you may find yourself short one member of the household, yet in possession of a superfluous chair, a second stove, a matching dresser. The fœtus sees merit in everything; this is why it brings joy to houses, with its innocence, and is loved by children, but this quality is also its defect. A fœtus will adore a book of matches, and seek to become it; if you do not arrive in time your expensive companion will proudly shape itself into the cheapest disposable. It is one thing to duplicate the crown jewels, quite another to become the owner of two identically stained copies of yesterday's paper, two half-full boxes of Kleenex, two phone bills.

We all know the fœtus's helpfulness and amiability, which became more and more apparent as it grew accustomed to our ways, and admire the dignity of the fœtus, which never fails it even when it is performing the most ignominious of tasks. No one was surprised when it came to be known as, variously, "Servus Servorum," "Husband of the Church," "Key of the Whole Universe," "Viceregent of the Most High," and, most colloquially, "Vice-God"; other nations may find it odd that our religious leader is of the same species as those creatures that well-off trendsetters purchase for their homes, but those who know better see no contradiction: the fœtus is born to serve.

The fœtus floats outside your window while you are having sex. It wants to know how many beads of sweat collect between your breasts and at what point, exactly, they begin their journey south, it wants to know if your eyes open wide or close at orgasm, if at that time your partner is holding your hand with his hand or your gaze with her gaze. It wants to know if your sheets are flannel or satin, if you lie on wool blankets or down comforters. And when fluids issue from the struggling bodies, with what do you wipe them up: Towels? Paper products? A T-shirt pulled out of the laundry? It wants to know if the bedside alarm is set before or after the lovemaking; it wants to stay informed, your love is its business.

The fœtus is here to serve us. If we capture it, it will do our bidding; we can bind its great head with leather straps, cinch its little hips tight. Then the fœtus willingly pulls a plow, trots lovers through a park, serves salad at a cookout. It does not scorn menial tasks, for to it all endeavors are equally strange, equally marvelous.

. . .

Only when it is time to make love must you bind the fœtus tight, lock it in its traces, close all the doors and windows. For at that moment the fœtus will rise in its bonds, larger and more majestic, and its great eyes will open and inside them you could see all of space rushing away from us—as it is! It is! The fœtus is sublime at that moment: set guards, and they will respectfully retreat; dogs, and they will lie down with their heads between their paws, blinking. And even if the fœtus is in tight restraint, you will feel it risen in your pleasure bed, the air will turn blue and burn like peppermint on your wet skin, and the shadows under the bed and the corners of the room will take on the black vastness and the finality of space. You will continue loving because that is our human agenda, what is set for us to do, though we know the fœtus whom we also love is suffering in its straps. Indeed, we make the fœtus suffer again and again, though we are full of regret and pity, and these feelings swell in our chests and propel us together with ever greater force, so we seem to hear the fœtus's giant cry, deafening, every time we slam together. We love cruelly, and in pain.

MELANCHOLIC

CANCER

The cancer appeared in my living room sometime between eleven and three on a Thursday. I am not sure exactly when, because I suffer from bouts of migraine, and sometimes I miss things, or see things that aren't there, flashing shapes like the blades of warrior goddesses, the vanes of transcendental windmills. A little airborne sprig could go unnoticed some while.

It was barely visible, a pink fizz, like a bloodshot spot of air. It was so small there was no great wonder in its hanging there, the way a feather might rest on an updraft. It is hard for me to admit it now, but when I first saw it, I thought it was pretty. I blew on it. It drifted sideways, but when I looked for it later, it was back where it had been before.

The cancer grew with improbable speed. At first I watched it curiously, almost fondly. Near the center it distended and grew as solid as meat. The branches divided and divided again. It was a starfish with split ends, an animal snowflake.

I did not speak of it to anyone. Once, the neighbor came to ask me to restrain my hedges. She was a nervous woman with a face too old for her hair. Her child was with her, that little blond creature I had once attempted to befriend. The child paid me no attention, but stared past me in the direction of the living room. I intercepted her gaze out of instinct, not any fear I could have named.

I looked at the cancer every day. Perhaps it was as big as a chicken—no, a parakeet—when I set my hand against it. I took one of its twigs and bent it back on itself. I did this out of curiosity, no more. When the tips darkened and began to wilt, I let go and looked up. The little girl was looking at me through the fogged window, her white fingers like claws on the edge of the sill. When she caught my eye she dropped out of sight. By nightfall the limb had straightened itself again, though it was a darker purple where the damage was.

We pop our kitchen sponges in a bath of bleach and dig the moldy grout from around the sink; it is the season for dentistry, manicures, and laser depilation. We rinse the food off our plates the minute we are finished eating, scrape the soft sludge into the garbage chute with a shudder of distaste. Everything soft seems decayed to us; we wear nylon jogging suits we launder daily, we cut our hair or pull it back into flawless chignons.

Of course I tried to oust the cancer, though I felt ashamed of myself as I jabbed it with the broom, trying to force it out the window. I had tied a kitchen towel around my head, as if I thought the cancer might tangle itself in my hair in its panic. What a figure of fun I seemed to myself, especially when the cancer proved impossible to budge! I should be more clear: it was possible to shift it, but something invisible bound it to the center of the room, and the farther it was from that point, the

more insistently it sought to return. (Not like an animal struggling, mind you. More like a buoyant object one tries to force
under water.) Finally, I trapped it in my apron—I also wore an
apron—and hobbled to the front door with it straining between
my legs. On the front porch I met the postman. We looked
down at the large mass struggling inside my apron. When I
raised my eyes, I was met by such a grotesquely knowing, indeed sympathetic gaze that I dropped my bundle and stepped
back, setting the door between us. After this I stopped trying to
evict the cancer. Besides, I had thought of something worse
than a cancer in my living room: a cancer tapping on my window, or leaning on my doorbell for all the world to see.

Another time I held a match to the tips. They curled into spirals, tight as watch springs, then turned to ash and fell off.

After the operation the little girl had stopped going to school.
She seemed to live in the yard. When she spotted me at the
window she stopped whatever she was doing until I went away.
She was always carrying something: a large piece of chicken
wire, a carburetor, a brick. I never saw her with a toy.

I knew that in some way I had secreted the cancer, sneezed
it from a nostril. It was not from outside. Every success it enjoyed was evidence against me. In it, you could watch my fault
take concrete form; it was a kind of malignant trophy. I thought
I could live with it, at first. It is some comfort to get what we deserve, even when we deserve nothing good. Perhaps I was
proud of my error, because it was so brightly colored, and took
such definite form. To have it was to have something, that was
certain. In private I might fit a ring onto one of its digits, a
gaudy ring with a yellow stone. I looked at it, you could almost
say lovingly: what lawless circus beauty. The stink of the big

cats, the glare of the lights! I forgot myself, brought my hands close, almost petting the hairy fringe. But afterwards ran scalding water on my palms.

I thought I could guess the size it would end up. But it grew and grew. It was the size of a badger, then a goat, then an ox. I compare it to animals because it was hot, as if blood ran through it instead of sap. Its body heat tropicked the room. And though it resembled a bush, I guess, more than anything else its own size, it had an animal presence, uncouth, yet sly, subtly critical, disturbingly womanly. If I looked away, and let my mind wander, I was brought back with a start by the feeling that someone was there.

Still, a great leafless bush, with smooth skin like the manzanita. The muscular trunk (it was hardly a trunk; the ganglion, rather) was scarlet. The limbs were streaked with purple, fading to pink toward the ends: pink fretwork against my ceiling. They grew thinner and more translucent, until it took a keen eye to make out where they no longer were. The air itself seemed stained.

We roll things, hard things, across surfaces, hard surfaces, because we have an unquenchable thirst for the clean sound of hard things hitting. We beseech the ovarian sky to let fall the rain it is thick with, we light lighters to purge the flatulent winds, we pull our bedsheets tight and our hospital corners have a truculent look that makes babies cry.

The feeling of plenty, of fruitfulness oppressed me. I seemed sunk in a fog of pollen. Breathing was heavy, repetitious labor, without hope of rest, like bailing water from a boat. The smell of bacterial abandon hung in my armpits. My hair was lank and tacky scant hours after I washed it. Yet I was in great health, my heart tolling in my rib cage, coppery new chest hairs sprouting amid the limp gray ones. I woke up hard every morning. To cover these signs, I began wearing a loose jacket and baggy trousers, though my style of dress before had been neat to the point of prim.

I gave her a ball once. When I first moved in she still had all her hair, and was halfway pretty, though already frail. She was somehow downy, covered with fine hairs, which were invisible until the light made a halo out of them. It was a hard, red rubber ball with a fine bounce. She took it without smiling. I looked out the window and saw her small, concentrated figure "at play" (if that is what play is). The ball bounced off the ground at the base of the wall, hit the wall, and raced back to her hands; she threw it again. As determined and joyless as a repairman banging a nail. All afternoon I heard the echoing blows of the ball, a double beat with a pause between. Then she was called inside, the blows ceased, and that was the end of them.

Perhaps the cancer was innocent of ordinary intentions on me. It was no footpad. Yet there was something brutal about its vitality. It was blazing with health, pert, straining apart at every fork. It was not merely visible: it exposed itself, and seemed to glory in my chagrin. It was like Rumpelstiltskin showing up in my living room looking for answers. No matter what I said, stomp stomp and through the floor he plunged in a brimstone stink, but he'd be back again another day, the hairy nymph.

The cancer grew bigger, until it was more like a place than a thing. I kept the door closed. I did not go into my living room for days on end. When my thoughts turned to it, my face went sour and I made a quick, involuntary utterance: "Never mind" or "I don't know" or "I don't want to." I began to see the cancer waiting behind every conversation: a lure, a magnet. I sought to avoid it and discovered myself summoning it up. My conversations were all evasion and omission: I hid things that had nothing to do with the cancer, but that I thought might, in the end, lead me back to the cancer, which was therefore not just a cancer in the world, but a cancer in language, a ruined area where nothing normal could come to pass. I'm going to be found out, I thought. At times the cancer hung so palpably behind me, a great red nimbus, like the radiance behind the sacred heart, that I would turn around and look. Or is that something I saw in a dream: a little girl with white hair and white eyebrows staring at me from the red corona?

Her face was hard and hollowed, cheekbones like a fashion model's, unpleasing on a little girl. Hard, ridged ears that stood out from her thin neck, parting her wispy hair. One day she was beating a tree with a two-by-four; the bark had gone fibrous and smashed, like a matted wig. She beat it rhythmically, deliberately. They had operated on her skull; there was a bald patch on the back of her head, with a triangular welt in it, like an octopus bite.

We dig under our fingernails with frightening insistence, troweling out tiny heaps of evidence. We use our teeth to chop at our cuticles until they bleed. Some people pluck their eyebrows, taking one hair from the right, one from the left, one from the right, from the left, from the right, and so on; then cry out in dismay. Hair is brushed until it frizzes, dreads are combed out and forked into great aureolae, or braided so tight our eyelids turn inside out. Manicurists and suppliers of facials batten.

· · ·

One day when I came home the girl was crouching at the side of my house, beside the chimney. I hissed and raised my arms suddenly from my shoulders, a great bird, and she bolted, wriggling into the hedge. Her thin, bleached legs stuck out for a minute, red shoes scuffling at the dirt; then they were pulled in after her. I saw that a few tendrils of red had emerged from around the loose metal ash door at the base of my chimney. I couldn't see her, but I could tell she was still inside the hedge, watching me from between the leaves. I felt her eyes on me as I unlocked the door.

I went in and forced the branches away from the fireplace. The floor was covered with ants. A few days later, it was a tarry, mauve substance that made my soles stick slightly when I walked. The backs of my leather books bloomed mildew white and green and the legs of my chairs grew fuzzy.

The cancer waxed stronger every day, every tendril a tine, metallic and purposeful. The yoke of every fork was swollen and fleshy. Tiny splits opened and leaked a purple ichor midges stuck in, and the smell was strong and sweet. At first the cancer had seemed to siphon water from the air like a hydrotropic plant, but one day I saw that one of its thicker roots had struck through the floorboards. I crawled under the house. The muscular trunk was sunk in the ground, spanning the gap between the floorboards and the earth, and it seemed to pulse slightly, as if something were passing through it, into or out of the house.

The sky looks like it hurts. We think about the way the sky looks and it frightens us. We think, What have I done to hurt the sky? *Some people walk around with their stomach muscles clenched and invite other people to punch them there. Some people punch them unnecessarily hard, there or somewhere else. We worry*

that delicate glass things, spun glass fawns and vacuum tubes,
may break of their own accord, and scatter floors with a crys-
talline, dangerous powder. People who are prone to nosebleeds
sit perfectly still while blood flows out of one nostril or both,
black as plums.

Once I opened the door and a white cat whirled around my legs
and disappeared into the kitchen. Later I saw it waiting under
a chair, watching me. When I opened the living room door
again it shot across the floor and through it.

Later I noticed the ash door was standing open. That was
how the cat got in.

Then one day I opened the door and the little girl was sitting
on a chair beside the cancer. She looked at me bitterly. I backed
out and closed the door.

The ends began to bend against the ceiling and walls—but I
don't know why I say this. I never went in there anymore. Perhaps I opened the door once, concerned for the child.

That last part is a lie. I detested the child.

One night I opened the lid of a casserole and found a steaming length of the cancer inside. It was strange and horrible to
see it, and the saliva rose in my mouth. I reached carefully between the forking tendrils, took hold of the firm trunk and
lifted it, the way you lift a lobster, and transported it gingerly to
the garbage. I looked away as I dropped it in. The little girl
must have crept into my kitchen and planted it there. If only I
could have urged her parents to restrain her.

I went for long walks alone. On one such, I stopped near a
playground. The sun had come out after a rainy night. On the
damp, dark concrete a group of boys were scuffling over a basketball, watched over by a gray-haired woman, a man with a

whistle clamped in his teeth. Behind the court, across a bit of green, was a row of blue benches. In the rain-brightened air the sound of the basketball rang out, and the peeps of the whistle pierced my ears like quills. Real people play such games as these, I advised myself. Watch and see how it is done.

I stuck my hands into my pocket. In the depths of it something rubbery seemed to squirm. I withdrew my hands as if—what's the phrase: stung? But nothing could have startled me more than that tentative, somehow fond snuggle. I felt again. Then plucked the tuber out and hurled it away from me. It bounced, even seemed to spring along from one limb to another, as if it were running, and shuddered to a stop next to the basketball court. A boy bent over it. The sight of the young body so close to that forked red thing was unbearable and I darted out across the playground, aware what a bizarre figure I cut in my giant pants, my flapping sleeves. I snatched the tuber. The boy fell back a step, his eyes on the thing I now held between two fingers, then he flipped his hair back and went back to his game. I carried the thing away the way you might carry a moth or a spider, making my hands a cage. I walked toward the blue benches. The woman and the man with the whistle were watching me. If I had been sure they had spotted the little red bouncing root I would have held it at arm's length, distastefully, as one might carry a dog's stool in a baggie, but that would draw attention to it, and perhaps they had not noticed it at all, but only my peculiar scuttle, in which case better to move my arms as naturally as possible.

When I came back, there was a turd on the center of my dining table. It glistened, and it was full of red bits like snips of rubber band.

I decided to take a walk out of the city altogether, to a field all itchy with grass seeds sifting down and bugs climbing up on the long stems. The sun bit into the back of my neck. Halfway across I got down as if forced to my knees. I smelled the heat in the dry grass, a blond smell. I sank my hands into the dry sheaves and suffered the bugs to walk up my arms. The blue vacuum above me sucked at the back of my head and made me feel strangely elongated. In contrast everything before me, bugs like tiny brooches, pods and plumes and burrs, was dense and small. I folded a hank of grasses around my fist and looked at the waxy stems lined up across the back of my hand. This is the real world, I said to myself. Pay more attention to it.

I dropped the grasses, and fell forward onto my hands. The earth was hard and deeply cracked. I strove my fingers into the earth. My fingertips grazed something smooth and the thought struck me, absurd as it sounds, that this was in some sense the jewel of the real, and would bestow on me everything I lacked: gravity, clarity, ruthless pragmatism. I started to dig, clawing at the sides of the crack. I lifted out the loosened dirt one handful at a time. The last revealed something red. I brushed the remaining dirt away. There in the cavity, twisting from the side into the cleared space, vital, acquisitive, was something I recognized. In the warm earth, coiling and humping in the darkness, the cancer had made its way to meet me.

It has gone under the ground, I thought. It might come up anywhere now.

Coddled tots will be given the root to suck. They'll open wide: their innocence will drop out like a tooth. Their face will redden with concentration and grow older, tiny daddies in diapers and jumpers will suck a pipe, aunts suckle a cigar. Such sweets are not for kiddies, I shall warn, a hilarious oldster with a bee in my

bowler. We will clip the fine ends and teacup them. A new brew
will sweeten the tongues of gossips, but what will they say in
their new voices, so high and so surgical?

The next morning I mused over my tea: possibly, I thought, I
could make my peace with the cancer. I approached the door
on stocking feet, opened it gently, smiling. The little girl had
crawled into the cancer, and was sitting on one of the limbs like
an owl, her knees drawn up. Her baggy stained underpants
confronted me. She was staring at me with that fixed look, like
a doll. I rushed to my room, and buried my burning face in my
pillow. After a while, I fell asleep.

When I woke up I found myself sucking on the broken end
of a branch. Had someone slipped it into my hand while I slept?
A sweet taste was in my mouth and there was some sediment on
my tongue, granular and faintly chalky, which made my teeth
feel unfamiliar. I was breathing peacefully through my nose. I
took the branch out of my mouth. I had hollowed out the cut
end with sucking. Crumbling and dissolving bits like tea-soaked
sugar tumbled out of it. The smooth skin was shiny with my
saliva.

I set the branch down on the bedside table and carefully ex-
tricated myself from the bedcovers. In the bathroom I brushed
and flossed, penitently, punitively, with a swollen heart. Then I
went to the room the cancer was in, axe in hand. The little girl
was still there. I hissed and darted at her. Reluctantly, she rose
and went to the fireplace, parting the branches before her with
her narrow white arms. The ash door stood open again. A
healthy child her age could never have fit through the door, but
she dropped to her stomach in the empty fireplace and went
right through it like a boneless thing, rocking from side to side,

humping along on her elbows once she was partway through. There was a glimpse of sunlight, her red shoe. Then the door clanged shut. The invisible ends played against my face.

I reached in and caught up a hank, swung the ax at the taut strands. They did not part as easily as I had pictured; I had to worry at them, sawing, and when they broke the ends leaped like elastic. One snapped against my cheek and brought a tear to my eye. I stepped inside the cancer, hacking around me indiscriminately. The limbs shook only with my own movements.

Branches fell around me, springing up again to clobber my knees and ankles. The insides of the thicker branches, once I split the sheath of fibrous rhubarb stuff, were pulpy and pink. It fell out in chunks from the cut ends. Only the red corm was left, rearing up in the midst of the wreckage. It was my height. I swung. The axe bit into the body and stuck, a heavy bad feeling. When I pulled it out, gobs of the inside stuff spattered my shoes.

I stood in a still heap of red lengths. There was silence in the room. A pink clot detached itself from the ceiling and dropped at my feet. I looked up at the dot of mucus that marked where it had been. Nearby, other clots trembled, unsticking themselves. They rained slowly down on the body, on the murderer. The clot at my feet was shrinking into a widening disk of clear liquid. There was no epochal shift, no grind of planets swerving in their spheres. I was still guilty, perhaps I had always been guilty, in advance, for this moment. I saw her face at the window, then it went.

NERVE

Me—who am as a nerve o'er which do creep
The else unfelt oppressions of this earth.
                                                    —Shelley

Completely normal, he wrote, *for man years completely normal,* then he took out *man* and put in *many.*

Maybe he had just spent too long working the nerves. Nerve fibers once had a reputation as aphrodisiacs, and were fashioned into amulets for daily wear, from simple rings and bracelets to elaborate knitted codpieces. In the town where George grew up locals believed to this day that a walk in the nerve fields made women ovulate and a handful of freshly cut nerve fibers under the pillow brought true dreams of love. A nap in the fields had more lasting consequences: George's town, like every small town on the Great Plains, had one or two children known as *nervous.* They were said to be the offspring of the plains themselves, and their mothers were blamed for nothing more damning than carelessness. Skeptical outsiders might take note of the many flattened patches in the fields near town, and the well-trodden paths that led to them.

Tender, susceptible fields! A careless boot sent a wave of consternation seven miles. A gunshot made the plains flinch to their last hummock. But at night, when lovers lay in congress in the fields, the pale strands flexed contentedly against the black sky. Concentric rings spread from their several centers and collided in elaborate interference patterns that made the whole plains hum a particular note. In the village they heard the note. They recognized it, they smiled, they fell back asleep. Or they worked out the harmony on their creaking beds. George used to lie awake, listening.

Completely normal, wrote George, though he remembered going to his mother and saying, "Mom, am I nervous?"

"No, of course not, what put that idea into your sick little head?" Mom had said, and what George remembered was that he was disappointed. So, a desire to be special, even then.

Completely normal, wrote George, then selected the phrase and rendered it in bold, as if to spite his own memory.

Cut nerves left lying on threshing floors drift and roll and wind up all aligned with the earth's magnetic field, like iron filings swayed by a magnet in a classroom experiment. (Bring a smaller magnet into the barn and watch them try to follow it!) But there are places where the magnetic field of the earth is disorganized, the ley lines tangled. Compass needles wag; carrier pigeons lose their way.

It so happened that a big nerve supplier built a warehouse in one of these places, and that George worked there. Big signs were posted all over the building: CLEAN UP AFTER YOURSELVES. ALL NERVES MUST BE BUNDLED. And simply, SWEEP. The workers were meticulous, by and large. All the same, it was bound to happen: a nerve slipped out of a bundle, slithered under a pallet, went unnoticed. In a few days, another one got away. After a while there were four, five, twenty-five scattered here and there around the warehouse: under tables, in cracks in the floor, snagged on splinters in the door frame.

Slowly, slowly, they were drawn together. Some moved like inchworms, humping up. Some like sidewinders. Some just slithered. They amassed: a pale, luminous pile in what moonlight found its way through the dusty windows.

Nerve fibers have a curious property. They organize themselves. They twine, knot, braid, lace, plait, mesh, splice. Some stringent ancient script takes over.

By midnight, a thick braid lay shining on the ground. (At home, George was sleeping quietly for the last time in his life.) Over the ensuing hours, more strands knotted themselves to it. They formed nosegays, posies, faggots. Sheaves and bales. (George slept on.) They twisted, coiled, fretted themselves together. (George woke up, took a hard-boiled egg out of the fridge, baggied it, shook some salt into the bag, set out early for work.)

A forked figure stood, took a bite of the apple.

George's key turned in the lock.

These spontaneous assemblages of sensibility are not just admired by aestheticians and teenage girls. One minute you're a man of business, the next you're writing sonnets to a squiggle of sore pasta, and your career can go to hell for all you care.

The warehouse supplied nerve fibers to top designers. George handled the overseas clients. He was a burly, well-spoken man, with clean, filed fingernails. Nobody would have pegged him for the sort to ditch the wife and kids (not yet an actual wife and kids, but a prospective wife and kids, real enough that he could almost see their tiny, resentful faces as they waved goodbye) and go in for pain and sequins. Nobody including him. But there he was, in love with a length of forked lightning.

How long was that going to last? But it changed everything. Afterwards, he found that he remembered his past differently. Isolated incidents suddenly strung themselves together into an argument, a prediction. Innocent objects started to phosphoresce. A child's *Rainy Day Fun Book* metamorphosed into a grimoire.

"Tie a Turk's head in a hank of nerves—four fibers will do. Give the nerves a turn to make a neck. Reserve two fibers for the arms. Twist the remaining two together to make the body of your nerve man or lady. When half of their length is still remaining, separate them to form the legs. Give them a little loop at the end so the dolls have feet to stand on. Keep your eye on them while you fashion their outfits—don't let them get away!

"Here are some easy outfits you can make. Cut a dress out of plain paper. Tape the nerve lady to the back side. You may want to draw a pocket or an apron on the dress. Your nerve gentleman does not need much clothing, but perhaps you will want to give him a natty bow tie! Cut it out of plain paper and give it a gay pattern with your crayons. How about polka dots? Or stripes? Now your nerve gentleman is ready to step out with the lady of the house.

"Maybe you would like to give your nerve man and lady a shoe-box house to live in. Glue a piece of patterned paper on the floor to make a rug. You can cut out miniature pictures for the walls, or draw windows for them to look out of. Chairs can be made out of corks and nails, see page 23. Do they like to watch TV? Draw a scene from your favorite TV program on the front of a box, and add some dials. Use your imagination!

"When you're finished playing, just put on the lid to keep them safe and sound until next time."

"It was cruel," George told his therapist. "But children are cruel, aren't they? Not evil, but nonchalant about pain. I was interested in salting slugs, swatting flies. Of course, the general opinion at the time was that the nerve dolls didn't suffer because they weren't really alive to begin with. Frog legs kick in the lab with no frog attached to them, you know. Chickens gad about without their heads.

"They weren't the best-looking dolls. No more than stick figures. Their paper-doll dresses hung crooked, and exposed their backsides whenever they turned around. How I laughed!

"Now I regret the bow ties and aprons. What an impertinence. The poor things were in agony. They were just alive enough to feel pain. A knot of appetite and no insulation. An erect twinge, a stitch on tiptoe.

"They waltzed, after a fashion, holding each other up so as little of them as possible touched the ground. Then they fizzed, smoked, fell over and 'died.' 'Boo hoo!' I cried, 'Boo hoo!' and held little funerals. That was my favorite part."

Not that pain is the worst thing in the universe. Interesting things happen when you adopt pain for your own. This thing you were prepared to spend your life flinching from is suddenly just another piece of information.

George began to feel that his own comfort was an affront. Sitting on the toilet, he squeezed the rolls of fat around his middle, cupped his breasts, measuring. Somewhere inside George was another George: spiderlike, avid, flexile. Like grammar, but physical. George wanted to make himself into this other George so that he would be more like his lover and by being like him, possess him again. So he ate less and less and during lunch at the warehouse he picked up some fibers and played cat's cradle with himself. When he could not help himself but eat, when it was someone's birthday and everyone sang and there were cupcakes with candles on them, he learned how to make himself vomit up the sweet sludge before it stuck.

Cat's cradle used to be a game for priests and princes. It retains a whiff of the sacred. You are playing a game with string, then you are in the milieu of the miraculous.

Every once in a while, through luck or incredible skill, a figure is actually perfect. An instant is long enough: the cat's cradle kindles. Flames run along the fibers. A glyph of fire stands in the air. It goes out a second later; all that's left is a blue smoke, a weird smell, a fading cicatrix on your retina. Your hands fall away.

"Everything perfect burns itself up," George told his therapist. "A perfect thing does not have to hang around, it has satisfied all the requirements of existing. That's what Deja says. Or maybe a perfect thing can't hang around, because perfection has no place in our world, which is a world of approximates. Existence *is* approximation; we are because of a kind of blurring of the material world. All attempts at perfection are destructive, therefore."

"Want to talk about this diet you're on?" said his therapist.
. . .

French designer Deja, one of George's best customers, had made the front-page news worldwide when his electric dresses burst into flames on the runway and disappeared in a puff of smoke, leaving two of his models naked and innocent of body hair.

"Well," shrugged Deja in newsprint, "it simply means I achieved a perfect form. Perfection cannot last." One model later revealed that she had not had any body hair to begin with. This had not stopped Deja, next spring, from bringing out a triumphant new line of depilatory dresses for ladies, depilatory culottes and tunics *pour l'homme*. "All have sold sensationally in Europe, but American customs officials have refused to allow them in the country. Yes, they are dangerous—so is *l'amour*, which recognizes no boundaries!"

George read the article to his therapist. "As yet, France is the only country where you may attend the opera with your head in flames, but American scene-makers were seen passing a petition at the Paris and Milan shows, so we may see a relaxation of the policy yet.

"Buyers have conveyed to Deja their customers' requests for depilatory panties that can be worn to work. 'Our customers love the idea of depilatory clothes, but are afraid to go to the office in a dress that may go poof,' they say. 'Many of our customers are successful women in high-paying jobs and must maintain a professional demeanor,' they insist. 'Unfortunately, naked says unprofessional to these women.' So far Deja is resisting the pressure, though underlings have dropped hints that he may soften his stance in time for fall. We spoke to him in his Paris atelier.

" 'Beauty must be convulsive or not at all, isn't it?' he says. 'I give the people something to look at, like it or not.'

"There was a flash of light and his pants disappeared. We saw what he meant."

"Boys don't do this," thought George, his soft breasts shrinking, parallel horizontal creases appearing in his stomach, a strange side effect of weight loss, his ribs appearing, knuckles appearing. "This is what girls do"; then he was filled with pity for girls, and admiration for their love of will over appetite.

George was no longer looking very much like himself, hair dry and wispy, bruises on his arms, a broken blood vessel in his right eye from puking too hard, eye flooded with cardinal red, the whites not white, closing in on the pupil, which stayed blue, however. Lapis and ruby. He tried to keep his eyes lowered until this condition passed, so as not to flash his single soiled petal, his damned spot. He was appalled but slightly thrilled by this disfiguring mark. He celebrated by burning off all his pubic hair with one of Deja's new samples. He was purifying.

A guitar can be strung with nerve fibers. It is difficult to play, since nerves stretch: every note bends. The sound is unearthly, instantly recognizable, and not to everyone's taste. It enjoyed a brief vogue in psychedelic music, then reestablished itself as a solo instrument, where problems of tuning are less evident. Very few modern pieces have been written for the nerve guitar, since the plaintive traditional melodies are so rich in variations and so difficult to master that most guitarists spend their lives learning to play them, and prize nuanced performance over an original tune. (Chanter Ramos, who in the seventies used to strap on a nerve guitar to head his fifteen-member band of multi-culti artistes, was a figure of fun to these musicians.) On stormy or sexy nights, when the plains hum, you can sometimes hear a solitary nerve guitarist start up a descant over the drone. There is no more piercing or desolate sound.

George had sneered at this music when he was a kid. Now it was the only true and necessary music for him. He listened to it on headphones while he worked.

"They call them 'nervous systems.' Baloney. They're people," George told his therapist. "The so-called *system* I fell in love with had more personality than I do. He loved tin lunch boxes, exotic weapons, tiny sugary cakes. He had delicacy and whimsy, but also the thirst for knowledge. Think Audrey Hepburn as Marie Curie: a pretty dress and a pocket full of radium.

"He was a kind of tuning fork. He vibrated with a perfect pain. I trued my pain to his and my pleasures fell into harmony as well. I had never felt so much, but it was nothing beside what he could feel; he was a perfect receiver. But you could see that for him, pleasure also hurt. There wasn't any difference, really, between pleasure and pain."

George got fired.

"It's not that you're not doing a good job, because you are. It's just that the other fellas find you ... unnerving." The boss had a good laugh, then clapped George on the shoulder. "Sorry about that!" He composed himself. "We like you, George, and it's good sensitivity training for the guys to learn to work with someone with your condition, but frankly you get on their nerves and—sorry! Sorry! And output suffers. I've got to ask myself what's best for the corporate body as a whole. I'm thinking it'll be better for you, too, in the long run. You'll be able to put in for unemployment, take a little break, change of pace. It's gotta be good to get out of temptation's reach—right?"

As he left, he heard someone mutter, "Nervous Nellie!" An

uneasy laugh rippled around the room. He put on his head-phones.

"One minute, a bundle of nerves, the next, they're demanding Purcell, performance art, the times of their lives," George told his therapist. "Oh, it's so hard to watch them, swaying and long-ing. They want to be ballerinas. They want to marry Bluebeard, be tempted, and rub and rub at the bloodstain on their finger. They ask for frocks, opium, a ruby—just one!

"They look nothing like us. They look like a gardener's ex-periment run to seed, they look like macrame sculptures. But they appreciate us, none better. They want to try taxidermy. They say, 'I've got stigmata!' They love Soutine, Ensor, tap dancing. They know how to live.

"They're not aliens. They are not animals. Give them a break! They are newborn, and terribly easy to hurt. Let them attempt the French horn, what harm can it do them? Give them typewriters. I'm seeing this now. I'm wishing I could have him back, start over. Ever read *Frankenstein*? I didn't give him the nurturing environment he needed. I was too, I have to use the word, unnerved."

"Why don't you go home for the holidays," his therapist sug-gested. "It's your birthday, too, isn't it; you're a December baby. You've got some free time now. Touch base with family. Con-sider letting them in on what you've been going through. It's a risk worth taking."

"It's that time of year again, and here's your friendly fireman to deliver our annual safety tip: keep nerves away from bare bulbs and candles! Nerve tinsel is only safe for trees without Christmas lights. It looks pretty, but it's a real fire hazard. The same goes for garlands. Nerve wreaths are safe, but wear rubber gloves if you weave your own, and don't hang them within reach of the little ones.

"Let's keep one jingle bell from ringing this December: the fire bell!"

"My word, that's a nice suit," said George's mother. "A bit flashy, maybe. But it certainly has a nice hang. You must have lost weight. You look gaunt. Have some birthday cake. George! Take off your headphones while I'm talking to you."

"I love you, wrecker of homes, ruination of family holidays," George wrote, "because you're a lightning rod, a perfect conductor for electricity and orchestras, a magnifying glass in the sun with a wisp of smoke sidling out from under it. You're a one-note solo that pierces our eardrums. You're a jungle gym heating up under the sun, branding our baby fat.

"I love you because flesh is stupid, like everything we build in imitation of the flesh: concrete blocks, sofas, airbags, all these hunks of dumb stuff that protect us. You're the cure for this sinus infection that stands in for a life, all the gluey textures of social intercourse and the bland obstructions. I'd carve off my own flesh in strips, leaving only the nerves, to spend one moment in pure apprehension. I want the skinny."

"How could you, George? I've never heard anything so ridiculous. This is just a story you've cooked up to try me in my old age. You look terrible, you look sick, you've got some crazy ideas in your head, they're probably hallucinations from not eating. Here. One slice is not going to hurt you, and I won't hear any more about this so-called love affair; you're just trying to shock me."

"I know this is unreasonable, that only a fanatic can't forgive the pileup of innocuous by-products of the life-well-lived. Matisse (the pure line, the untempered aquamarine) compared a painting to an armchair, and Dickens made people laugh. I know the guru on the mountaintop is just a cartoon. Real life is lived in the details, the plastic Teletubbies cups and the bottle resealers that don't quite work. We drop dead cells by the billions and go racing on in a flurry of dandruff, we fill holes with empty Yoplait containers, there is no economy to our carrying on, nor should there be. I suspect that only the comfortable value pain. But I want a short, arachnid life of art and acrobatics and leave the curds and whey to others. I want a life like a squib: one sizzle and I'm out."

"For me? It's not *my* birthday." She ripped the paper off. "Well. Now that's what I call a hat. Where did you get your sense of style? Certainly not from your father. When will I have any chance to wear something like this out here in the boondocks? It certainly is elegant, though—"

"Don't try it now, Mom. Mom! Don't—"

After they had extinguished the blaze, and Mom had settled her second-best wig on her head, pointedly allowing the once best to sizzle on in the kitchen sink, George went to the upstairs bathroom and rid himself of the cake, making no attempt to keep the noise down. Then he went out. He walked to the edge of town, grinding his teeth gently together, reflecting on how the freshly acid-washed enamel made this more of a rubbing than a sliding sensation, and subtly unpleasant. He crossed the drainage ditch, stepping onto what looked like a solid bank, and his right shoe filled with icy water. The cold began to wick up his wool sock. Right, notice everything, he told himself. Pain and pleasure. Better to burn up than to fade away.

An image came to him of the nervous system—no, his *true love*—standing by the bed, his head in flames. He suffered this image to remain, though a tiny sound broke from him; he heard it as if it were someone else's. Darling, his lover had signed, smiling, insofar as he could be said to smile. Oh, that was the killer, he didn't know he was burning. It was all one to him: flames, George's touch, a breath, laughter, death. What George felt about this: pity. Guilt. Also envy.

George passed among the nerve fibers in his birthday suit, going in deeper.

It could happen, thought George, he could rise again. A scattering of fibers that missed the hopper at harvest, a tidal wave of magnetized particles from the sun, a brief disturbance in the fields, and he could come again. Love's an accident waiting to happen.

The field began to hum.

D I L D O

Being Excerpts from: A DISCOURSE CONCERNING DIL-
DOES: WHEREIN FALSE CONCEPTIONS ARE REPRE-
HENDED, AND THEIR TRUE AND PROPER ENDS
ASSERTED AND VINDICATED. THE SECOND EDITION
CORRECTED AND INLARGED. TO WHICH IS ADDED A
GENERAL HISTORY OF DILDOES. WHEREIN SOME
CHARACTERS OF DISTINCTION BETWEEN TRUE AND
PRETENDING DILDOES ARE LAID DOWN AND BY MANY
THOUSANDS OF EXAMPLES IS SHEWED WHAT THE
DILDO HATH BEEN FROM THE FIRST AGES OF THE
WORLD TO THESE TIMES. IN RESPECT OF HIS BODY,
SENSES, PASSIONS, AFFECTIONS: His Virtues and Perfec-
tions, his Vices and Defects, his Quality, Vocation and Profes-
sion; and many other particulars. Collected from the Writings
of the most approved Historians, Philosophers, Physicians,
Philologists and others, by ANONYMOUS, London: Printed for
F. Basset, at the Rose and Crown in St. Paul's Church-yard,
1678.

Epilogue

What is a dildo? The question is very obscure, according to Paterculus, full of controversy and ambiguity. Saith Dandinus, I confess I am not able to understand it; we can sooner determine with Tully, what they are not than what they are.

In former times, the Sadducees denied that dildoes existed. So did Galen the Physician, the Peripatetics, even Aristotle himself, because they never saw them, and if any man shall stoutly maintain that he hath seen them, they account him a timorous fool, a melancholy dizzard, and a dreamer, and yet Ummidius of his credit told Psellus that he had once seen one. And Leo Soup, a Frenchman, will have the world to be as full of them as flies, and that they may be seen, and withal sets down the means how men may see them.

Wecker relates of his father that after the accustomed solemnities, in 1491, 13 August, he conjured up seven dildoes, some ruddy of complexion, some black and saturnine, and some pale. The same author will have some of them to be desirous of men's company, very affable, and familiar with them, as dogs are; others again to abhor them, as serpents do.

Fiery dildoes or *dildes fatui* lead men often into rivers or precipices, saith Lipsius, whom, if travelers wish to keep off, they must pronounce the name of God with a clear voice, or adore him with their faces prone on the ground. Likeways these sit on ship masts, and never appear but they signify some mischief or other to come unto men. The Polonian Duke calls this apparition the Heavenly Brothers. The King of Sweden had an enchanted dildo, by virtue of which he could command spirits, trouble the air, and make the wind stand which way he would, insomuch that when there is any great wind or storm, the common people are wont to say, the king has on his conjuring dildo.

Of a woman's fair hand, which rose out of a lake, holding a shining dildo, we read in many of the Ancients, such that it may not be doubted; and to this dildo many noble deeds are credited, many a citadel vanquished through its unimpeachable might, etc. And again of a dildo we read, which appeared to the daughter of the melancholy Duke of Cleve in a dream, which was so beautiful, that upon waking she pined for it, and tore her hair, and could not be comforted, and her only recourse, though that unavailing, was to sleep, and hope the dream would come again; this dildo really existed, as Necromancers learned, but in far foreign lands, but the Duke so loved his daughter, that he set out on a quest, in great peril of his life, and bested many monsters, as is told in the Epic, to win the dildo and bring it back to her, and when she beheld this apple of her eye, she sat up in bed completely cured. And Weenus tells of a lady that so loved her dildo, that she begged to marry it, and when the pope spoke against it, she ran mad, and dressed in rags, and fled to the greenwood, and there lived in sin with her paramour. There are also sad tales of dildoes who fell in love with their keepers and were given horns by mortal lovers, and humorous tales of dildoes in nunneries that went limp at last from surfeit. In Eastern parts, as travelers tell, a certain dildo was recognized by infallible signs as a reincarnated holy man, and was dressed in fine robes and gold dust was put on its head and it was treated with all honor once paid the man himself, and gave comfort to many and, some said, cured women suffering from melancholia and other nervous afflictions.

There is a foolish opinion, which some hold, that dildoes are mortal, live and die, that they are nourished and have excre-

ments, that they feel pain if they be hurt (which Dr. Guin confirms, and Rivet justly laughs him to scorn for), and, if their
bodies be cut, with admirable celerity they come together
again. The cautious Godefridus sets this condition, that the
dildo must in such cases be possessed, for that this does occur
is common knowledge, and also well set forth in reliable Histo-
ries by Gellius and others.

A dildo may be made of air, as Suetonius confirms, which is
a supple and lasting substance, and a very gentle fricative; it
may be of coal, or hammered copper, in which case the inferior
workman may yet prove the better friend, for what delights in
a candlestick may disappoint in a dildo, says Busbequius, as
cited by Pigiron, namely delicacy, sheen, and regularity. A dildo
may be of fired clay and sprung from a catapult, "at a fixed or
moving Target—very moving," as the wag Pistol has it. It may be
of clotted cream or curl papers. A lead dildo is called a Dutch
uncle, a dildo proceeding unnoticed past a sentry post is called
a silent partner, a dildo spoken about but not yet seen is called
a summons-to-court or a man-about-town. A wicker dildo is
popular in equatorial climates, as Kornmannus relates, and this
is called a windlass or an airy fairy. Nicknames for dildoes are
too numerous to list here; some in common use are: dried had-
dock, Welsh rarebit, gay blade, abigail, alderman, woodpecker,
bum steer, bedpost, and beau-nasty.

A blue dildo is for remembrance, a red one for ruth, the rare
silver dildo is for the first-born son on reaching his majority. In
ancient texts it may be seen that a dildo of Moroccan leather is
suitable for a lady of the merchant class, while her husband
may sport one of Cordovan leather. If it be made of pigskin, the
lady is said to be "high on the hog." Gentlewomen, however,
use ivory if their husbands can afford it; often this becomes an

heirloom, passed down from mother to daughter, kept in pride of place above the mantel, and passed over while many another ancestral treasure is borne away to be sold. Often these are finely figured, in low relief, though this practice is condemned by the stern Schottus, who calls it "a vanity, a species of idolatry, and injurious to the liver." A charming variant with an ancient history is the little horn dildo, imprinted with the alphabet in upper and lower case, the nine digits, and the Lord's Prayer. A hole was bored through the handle, and a cord was inserted so that the dildo could be hung from the neck, wrist, or waist.

The little dildo in daily use may seem like a distant relation of the ancient stone dildoes engraved with the names of dead kings that are still standing in parts of Abyssinia, but this range of uses and styles is intrinsic to the dildo. A dildo may be somber as a memorial statue, or playful and quick as a minnow. It may come together in an instant like a surprising sound and then dissolve. It may be made of pride, or compassion, or catgut, it may lace up or inflate. A tree stump used as a dildo will later sprout. A man's parts make a fine dildo, as Pompon stiffly maintains, and Bonius the Jesuit concurs. A doll may be a dildo, or a pillar of salt; there are dildoes of wrought iron, of brick, of water, of stitched horsehide packed with straw, of knotted string, ink, and ice, of gears turned by a tiny water wheel, of hint or innuendo, tar, sugar, and sal ammoniac, of vanity, of lamb's wool, of pig's bladder, of giant blocks of sandstone smoothed by the passage of time, of stuffed tapirs, sundials, mirrors, or bridges. A dildo may be blown out of glass. A charm or a coin may be sealed inside; ask a glassblower how this is done. A model ship may be tweaked erect inside the dildo by means of threads. This signifies the voyage that is sex, and the danger of capsizing. A memory of a lover is also a dildo, however fleeting. Be careful when you say the words *mildew, Bilbao, bibelot, billet-doux,* or even *peccadillo,* that you do not accidentally summon a dildo, for truly, you do not know what will answer your call.

Index

dildo

baffling malice with ready answers, 41–42

in battle, 79, 83, or gladiatorial combat, 81

bridegroom accidentally but fatally wounded by bride's dildo on wedding night, 28

brought to life by immersion in water, holy water, milk, blood, 65

called for by girls about to be executed, 49

Debates between Bodie and Dildo, 99

desired by pregnant women, 46

diminutive, but nimble, defeats huge and dangerous antagonist, 181

displayed, to embarrass a gallant, 202 *n.* 7

and dowsing, 99

emits blood on being approached by murderer, 162

enchanted, returned to human form by gaining girl's love, by being admitted to maid's bed, by a kiss, 4, 64, 72–73

enchanted, which will serve four-and-twenty maids at once, 137

euphemisms for, gude neighbor, good damsel, auld wee man, 191 exhibited, as token of conquest of mistress's virtue, 38

fathers nine pups, a pig, and a boy, 127

girl sold for a, 26, 205 *n.* 18

given back to dying man by maid, 32

halved by husband and wife at parting, serves to identify
    husband or lover returned after long absence; parts join
    of themselves on meeting, 29, 142

hung at every corner of a ship, 61

its love for the body, 104

as king's ransom, demanded by fairy queen, by Elfin
    Knight, 156–57

knight obliges lady to go off with him by sticking dildo in
    her sleeve, 35

laid in bed between man and woman, 28

made from drowned maid's bones and skin, or from reeds
    or tree into which drowned girl had grown up; tells of
    murder, 107–10

made of hot iron, as punishment for infidelity, 31

milk-white, four-and-twenty, demanded by bride, 88

as murder weapon, "daubd wi blude," 168

nix flies from, 42

og den lille Pigge, Danish, 32

or ring, choice given to maid, signifying death of violator or
    marriage with him, 62

and the Pricke of Conscience, 179

propounds riddles, 68–69

ridden by witches, 165

running with milk, 74–75

sea king's daughter has one of sixty ells length, 93

secret revealed to, after oath of silence, and overheard,
    33, 61

sent to jailor as warrant of queen's authority, 197

shot six score paces (three score rod, a hundred rod, two
    north country miles and an inch) to cleave apple on
    boy's head, 2, 4, 162–63

straking troth on, three times, 31

thrown into woman's lap controls her will, 128, 220 *n*. 6

transformation of, into beautiful lady, youth, linden-worm,
    king's son, fish, wolf, ugly worm, lost lover, fiend, fause
    knicht, 20, 136–37, 150, 164, 168, 179

used to draw a man out of a well, 182

whetted on straw, grass, a stone, the ground, wiped or dried
    on sleeve, grass before using, 2, 21, 29, 56

which by rusting or dimming shows giver is dead, 68

"with ae stamp o the melten goud, another o silver clear,"
    63, 178

wrung in grief, 32

Shortly after the printing of the first edition a warrant was is-
sued for "Francis Basset, Stationer" for the publication of this
"immoderate and deranged" work. Basset was imprisoned and
lost his shop and two years of trade. It cost him some three
hundred pounds before he was able to prove that he "had not
any knowledge nor never heard of it, contributed to it, read it,
nor delivered it out."

PHLEGMATIC

PHLEGM

Ever known an ugly girl who gets all the love she needs? I'm that girl. My coworkers at Adventurous Electrolysis call me the little tramp. It is true that I would look a bit like Charlie Chaplin if I wore a false mustache, and my walk is not unlike his. But they mean something different when they call me that.

I am one of those women who must know exactly in what ways she is presentable, in order to make the most of them, for they are few enough. I have a hooked nose and when I said I would need a false mustache to do Chaplin I did not mean to imply that I have no mustache of my own. At least, I would have, were it not for the perks of my place of gainful employ. All the same I have been called a handsome woman, with snapping black eyes. I have never liked the phrase. Handsome says to me that I have a magnificent bosom and a fine head of hair, but a big chin. I have none of the above, and if eyes snap it is an unseemly affair and I want no part of it. Furthermore, my eyes are hazel. But there you go. It is nice to be complimented at all.

Still, I know how to use the little I have, my flat stomach and rather flatter chest, my slightly bowed, but strong and flexible legs. I produce plenty of phlegm. I have clever hands and a stare that could take the silvering off a mirror. Men flatter themselves they are original in admiring me. How confused they are when they find out they have competition. (There is no desperation like that of a lover who has decided to do you a favor, and finds himself waiting in line.)

I like the way they think of me at work. They ask my advice on molding and flow. I lie. They suck it up.

My coworkers think I am really in touch with my phlegm. Not true. In bed, yes, I know what to do. [See Appendix 1.] I produce my handful, the electrician makes his contribution, we tweak and probe and despite ourselves he and I (two homely, difficult specimens) make something I am not ashamed to keep on the mantelpiece. This, phlegming's fabled peak, is easy for me. It's the rest that baffles me, the how do you do, and can I offer you some kirsch?

I have always felt that everyone else knows something I don't about phlegm. (Maybe if Mother had been around to explain, things would have been different.) Everyone else feels no qualms about sharing their phlegm with all and sundry, comparing textures and quantities, describing the changes it goes through as it ages and the best ways to groom it and skim off dust and insects; they vie to confess their doubts about their ability to produce the best phlegm, or keep producing phlegm, or produce it in sufficient quantities, or at the right time; they talk about molding and shaping it, whether it is acceptable to use cookie cutters, whether free-form modeling is more creative than strict formal arrangements. Every mail brings sticky little sentimental cards and gooey care packages from back home; turn on the TV and you'll see politicians holding up their gummy fingers, triumphant sports stars stretching a translucent cord between their raised fists, picture-perfect parents leaning over a crib with improbably large bubbles of phlegm hanging from their faces; in the tabloids pale starlets battle through green maelstroms to make Opening Night, phlegm dripping between their D-cups. You would think our economy ran on phlegm, which while private seems to belong to everyone, such that phlegm-withholding between husband and wife is considered a crime in some states, and at least a social blunder between friends and business associates, while the phlegm-challenged are everywhere pitied and also mocked. And yet it nauseates me.

After the thumb incident, the nursing home wanted nothing to do with Father. What could I do? I took him home. Every morning I hoist him out of bed. (He's not helpless, but he forgets what he is doing, and he is stubborn.) When he is dressed and has his bib on, we make the slow voyage to the kitchen. He greets his chair. He sits in his chair. All day, he sits and looks out the kitchen window. At night, back we go.

My father bangs his glass on the table and demands kirsch. "Kirsch!" It is all he will drink. My father was a swinging exercise instructor in the seventies. In the hall there is a photograph of him in leotards and a lab coat, the leotards for ease of movement, the lab coat to underline the medical soundness of his procedures. He has hair. He has his thumb inside a woman's mouth. She has a large behind.

What is he doing? He is applying pressure to the roof of the mouth to ease sinus pressure, nosebleeds, headaches, and hiccups. Every morning he shuffles past this picture, stops, turns back, and peers at it, as if he does not know what it represents. Who is that darkly handsome mustached man, and what is he after in there? Every morning he tells me, "I used to receive kiss-o-grams from grateful whatchamacallits, clients, ladies with large keisters. They liked the cut of my jib." Then he weeps. Every morning the grief is brand-new. He does not remember the grief of the day before. He remembers the kiss-o-grams, however.

One morning he dressed himself in his leotards. It was a sorry sight. His jib is shrunken and wobbly. Now all he wears is that damned kirtle. And the bib.

My father has dribbled kirsch on his bib, but there is no point in changing it now, so close to dinnertime. I pluck the stew meat from the pot. I put it in the grinder. Father can bite, but his hinder teeth are too rotten to chew, and I will not buy him baby food, not yet. So I make him his dinner: a sort of paste of meat and vegetables. Grout, I call it. I smear it on his teeth and he sucks it off. He does not thank me.

Father is dry, though I have always suspected he keeps back his phlegm on purpose, in habitual, petty ill will. My own flow has always been steady. However, my phlegm does not come for Father. Even when he is at his best, with his nose wiped and a glass in his hand, looking quietly out the window, my heart is hard against him. When he is most to be pitied, I stiffen, as if against a hand raised to strike. I have no more than the usual reasons to hate him; I should not begrudge him his little trumped-up self-congratulations now that he can be congratulated for so little. The traits for which my mother left him I know now were nothing special. His demands, his cries—well, I too once cried, once demanded. But still I have no phlegm for him. Not that he wants any. He wants for nothing.

Almost nothing. There is that touchy issue about the thumbs.

My boss is low-phlegm, but he works with it. He's slick at palming a prepared blob of phlegm (or *FLEM!*™) and pressing it into a new client's hand, to jump-start the camaraderie. Studies have shown this works even when you're conscious of the deception, so sophisticated types (he likes to think he is one) use colored and scented phlegm to make an impact while drawing attention ironically to the artifice. [See Appendix 2.]

"God knows phlegm production is not the be-all and end-all here at Adventurous Electrolysis. We're a reputable business. God knows we hired you in that you are highly skilled and not for your pretty face."

We laugh good-naturedly.

"But we need to talk about your people skills. Our customers want to see a little phlegm. Give to get!"

I stop listening. My boss molds phlegm with too much zest and alarms our clients, some of whom are skittish to begin with. You cannot tell him anything about phlegm, however.

My father wants me to put my thumb in his mouth. He says that if I will only do this, putting pressure on the palate, it will ease the chronic blockage he suffers due to his deviated septum. He begs me to do it. I have a problem with this: I am afraid he will forget himself and bite my thumb off. He would put his own thumbs in his mouth but he has no thumbs anymore, only the pads and those poor, futile flippers. He weeps.

. . .

When it is a matter of putting your fingers inside someone's mouth, accidents will happen. Father claims that two patients bit off his thumbs (on separate occasions): a blonde with hiccups and a nervous mother of four with a large keister. He says he remained calm and urged them to disgorge his thumbs. What a stroke of bad luck that they both had strong swallow reflexes! They tried to puke, he tried to make them puke, the EMTs with their ipecac tried to make them puke. Eventually they puked. But the thumbs were not fit for reattachment anymore. That was the end of his practice and the tragedy of his life. He weeps.

In fact he bit them off himself, possibly to protest the home I put him in.

Some of our busybody neighbors (led by Mrs. Nachtsheim, who also instituted the Block Watch and the Phone Tree), not content to let things take their course, have taken to spreading their extra phlegm outside their houses and encouraging others to do the same as a way of binding us closer together. The idea is that the autonomic processes of phlegm production will respond to this climate and take over, upping yield. Sometimes I see skeins of phlegm draped among the hedges in our neighborhood, but usually by midday it has dried into an almost invisible and barely tacky film that tears, shrivels into threads, and blows away. However, lately I have seen bigger blobs (under bushes, in the crawl space under porch steps) that last almost all day.

Father is kittenish today. "Check out the keister on her!" He is talking about the fat-bottomed woman across the street, who is carrying a limp swag of hose across the lawn. Her cat watches from the window with an air of affront. Halfway across the lawn the woman stops. Then she drops the rope as if she has forgotten it and walks back into the house. Has she thought of something better to do? Has she lost faith in the value of homely tasks such as watering the lawn? For a moment, when I saw her carrying the hose, I felt a slight uplift of the spirits, though I am only aware of it in the peace that comes afterwards, when familiar despair sweeps back in and puts things to rights, like a good nurse. I believed that she knew what she wanted of that hose, and she knew it was a right thing to want it, and she knew how to get it. It gave me a brisk, optimistic feeling about doing things when ordinarily doing things is not my strong suit. I was ready to try doing something myself, buying a little shovel maybe, with which to keep the driveway clear of phlegm if it should come to that. Of course she drops the hose, as I might have known she would.

Father sees things in a completely different light. He is unusually animated. I suppose I should be grateful for her keister. "Chyesss!" he says. He bangs his palm on his kneepan with a jaunty, yo-heave-ho sort of gesture. He attempts that pumping gesture baseball players make as they start around the bases, a gesture I find particularly repellent. I confess I feel some satisfaction when he bangs his elbow on the standing ashtray (now used as a spittoon). He weeps.

It seems that we may be about to go to war over a point of etiquette. The headlines, in quick succession, have read:

Diplomat Spurns President's Phlegm
Envoy "Wipes" After Formal Greeting

Ally Takes a "Wipe" at US
88% of Americans Hate Phlegm Withholders
Diplomatic Relations Collapse: US Won't Stand for Snub
War?

As a result it has suddenly become not just unfriendly but also unpatriotic to keep your phlegm to yourself.

Father is lonesome, though he would not admit it. Every time the phone rings, he perks up. For Father there are no wrong numbers.

We get a lot of calls. That is because of the Nimnick situation. I assume these callers, always foreign, are clients or customers, since they always ask for "Mr. Nimnick" or just "Nimnick"— Barney Nimnick is unheard of, as is Lance, Joachim, or Ulrich— and since they ask for him with such bright expectancy, but are not very disappointed not to reach him.

Occasionally, though, someone does seem disappointed, even distraught, and keeps repeating "Nimnick, Nimnick," unable or unwilling to grasp that he has moved on. Then I am full of a mellow astonishment and I remind myself that even a Nimnick stirs the deepest feelings in somebody's heart, if only in the heart of another Nimnick. A little phlegm comes up. But at this my heart changes again, and I am affronted, and turn away the caller with particular violence:

"There is no Nimnick! There has never been a Nimnick at this number!" And I hang up.

At Adventurous Electrolysis we have a little accident and have to call the electrician. The boss takes the singed client for a

really nice meal and to get him soused plus whatever it takes
not to get sued. I take the electrician home with me, as I have
done before. Not since Father came home, however. Father
bleats from his room but I ignore him. The electrician gives me
a questioning look but I press my chest up against him and he
relaxes.

Unfortunately, Father's cries put me in a weird frame of
mind. The electrician is shy and he waits to see what I will do,
breathing noisily. I wait too, lying up against him with my meager chest against his and my chin in the soft spot at the pit of his
neck, and I feel his ribs moving uncomfortably as he breathes,
and with my lips I feel his Adam's apple, and with my feet the
weird shapes of his feet against mine. In the hot space under
my chin a mucous ball suddenly forms.

I bring it forth and we play with it. [See Appendix 3.] We
smack it with improvised paddles, we smite it with ideations
and then we bring out our special tricks. I do the one that is like
winding a tetherball around a pole, the electrician does the one
that is like making a little paper hat for his finger and performing Punch and Judy. We play peek-a-boo through a "cooch" in
the phlegm. He "parks" his phlegm in my "domain," I fashion
a small symbolic torus for him to wear. We do poodling, purl-
ing, beading. When all is done, I am left with a souvenir in the
warm hollow of the bed, a little totem or statuette. It's not much
to look at, but I like it.

There are photographs of me, too, a square and dogged figure
in the "ethnic" shirts and wraps my mother saw fit to send me
to school in. I look something like a kachina doll, only not so
fetching. Mother looks regal in her kaftan, of course.

That was when Father was emulating Malcolm X and reading the dictionary straight through from start to finish. He had only gotten as far as K by the time Mother left us. "If only I'd had the whole dictionary under my belt, I might have been able to talk her out of it!" he said in a lucid moment. "I was taking my time, really trying to get to know *beargarden*, a rowdy or noisy scene, and *bertha*, a deep, falling collar often of lace, and even spending some time with words I thought I already knew, such as *Bermuda shorts* and *bestiality*. I hadn't gotten to *marriage* yet, I hadn't plumbed its glinting depths, its complex and shifting layers." He weeps. "All I have left is a few bobby pins with blond hairs caught in them, her kirtle, and you, our little kelpie."

"Whose fault is that?" I say.

Father says, "Why are you so uncompassionate? My gut tells me that our experimenting with lifestyles was to blame."

The neighbors congratulate one another when another phlegm bubble takes shape in our airspace, they compare notes on its extent and agree that it's bigger than the last one. They wonder how long it will last this time: twenty minutes, an hour, an afternoon? Eventually, it bursts, but someday it may not burst. Then it will slowly fill with phlegm.

I climb up on the roof with a long metal spike. It was once part of an umbrella. I have sharpened it. I lash it to the chimney. I hope it looks like an antenna. Of course its purpose is to pop the bubble, if it comes too close to my house. Mrs. Nachtsheim brings a delegation to speak to me about it. They suggest that there is something un-American about the spike, with respect to the international crisis. They hold out their hands. If I presented phlegm it would ease their minds, I know. But with a great effort I withhold; my vents stay dry. All day I feel excited and proud.

"Is Mr. Nimnick there?"

"He has not lived at this address for a long time."

"Mr. Nimnick, please?"

"Not here. No Nimnick."

"Nimnick?"

"No."

My boss stops by my desk and winks and makes a veiled reference to the electrician. "You're doing swell. Just remember to sow where you reap and what side your bread is buttered on! Don't hide your phlegm under a purely personal bushel, for goodness' sake!"

The phlegm I made with the electrician has dried and hardened into something not very nice. Cracked, disfigured. A sort of voodoo doll. All the same, it is a trophy of sorts. A green freak for the mantelpiece. I enjoy looking at it, and I even take it in my backpack to show my coworkers, though when I see it with their eyes I can't help saying things like, "It's got a lot of hairs stuck to it," and "I just did it because what the hell." Alone, I run my fingers over the ugliest bits. I smile and smell my fingers.

It is proper to mention the freak to the electrician. Not because he owes it anything; it exists now, separate from either of us, like a standing wave. I wouldn't want to see him brandishing ownership papers or even standing with a proprietary hand on the freak. But because I like it, I feel a rush of warmth toward the electrician. It is not necessary to confess that I hadn't expected so much from him, only to convey my pleasure that our accidental and ill-considered project came out so well.

The electrician welcomes me more enthusiastically than I expected. A ball of phlegm forms at my throat. I show the electrician. He palps it knowingly. I feel a faint revulsion, and begin to move away. But I check the impulse. I liked the freak. I might like the freak again.

Sometimes I think that a good daughter would let her father bite her thumbs off, or at least would not hesitate to perform the sinus-draining boon he craves (possibly wearing a protective thumb-guard such as one might devise from a piece of sheet metal and some wire, or maybe shoving a block of wood between the jaws, as wise heroines do in the case of dragons), but then I think, what is this self-defeating shit? How is it selfish if I elect to keep my thumbs, which are opposable and therefore help me to wield moist towelettes and keep the chin of my father in pink, shining good nick?

But I'm not entirely comfortable with this thought process, because as I have discovered through being involuntarily inducted into the caring professions, it is possible to do or say something entirely fair for self-serving and mean reasons. Though whether that implies that you ought to do unfair things so as not to be trying to come across so saintly all the time is not something I can quite weigh out on my moral scale. Is it better to help someone when you don't really give a hoot, or to refuse help because it's more honest?

· · ·

It must be hard to bite off a thumb. How fierce and vital Father must have felt as he chowed down. For one moment of decision and purpose. Then to relax back into lethargy and regret, forever.

This ennobles him in my eyes. Despite all the scorn and loathing he inspires, in the end he escapes my judgment. Unknowable, thumbless, he sits just out of reach.

Where Father's thumbs were there are ugly keloid cushions. It is sad to watch the stumps strain inward toward the palm when Father is trying to pick something up. When I look at the stumps vainly trying to help, I almost feel my phlegm come up. I even resent his stumps for being so cute and pitiful, since Father made them that way, probably on purpose to make people care for him, having taken a good gander at himself in the mirror and judged rightly that there would be no more free gifts.

The electrician and I go to bed again. We toil, and produce a scant dram of goo, a sorry gob. We start to play with it. It gets all over me.

Suddenly I am claustrophobic. I rip the hairs off my arms getting unstuck. (Oh, the involuntary depilations I have undergone.) The electrician collects a little phlegm off his own neck and sits there in his socks, molding it. Papa is wailing. Everything is terrible.

There is an area some blocks away where two or three houses and their inhabitants have become more thickly engrossed in phlegm. This is heralded as an occasion for civic pride; we received a flyer anouncing a celebratory potluck.

I have bought a shovel.

. . .

I decide that I will phlegm no more. The electrician is history and I will shake hands dry, never mind if I start World War III. I will bathe my slit with alum. If necessary I will tape it shut.

Now I spend a lot of time looking out the window with Father. We watch the woman with the big butt putter in her garden. Her red windbreaker is bright against the loogey building high over Loyal Heights; the verge of the congested area is only two blocks away now. Her shoulders are hunched.

"Sad woman," says Father. "Not a gardener. But what a keister."

My boss speaks to me again. "I'm talking outreach. A little sass and spirit of play will carry the day here at Adventurous. I have to stress that while I wouldn't go so far as to say your job is in jeopardy—" I zone out until he sticks his hand right under my nose.

"Let's try this. It won't hurt. Put 'er there, tenderfoot!" I look at the nonstandard white phlegm laid out on his palm ready for some companionable manipulation, the comment-inspiring white phlegm, with its Crisco good looks. "Cross my palm with phlegm, pal!"

Sometimes I still think I am wrong, a little glad-handing never did anyone any harm. I think, *This "phlegm," what is it?* Only a social convention. Only a ritualized transaction through which the tribe reaffirms the bonds of kinship, convenience, and casual domestic disgust that hold it together. Without which we would all fear and suspect one another.

But then I remember: we do fear and suspect one another.

. . .

I have been phlegm-free for weeks. I feel thin and brisk and clear-sighted. I wipe Father's nose with unnecessary vigor and brook no complaints. I avoid my boss. I am examining the phone bill, on which some unfamiliar numbers appear, when there is a knock at the door.

I open the door. A corpulent man with an ID tag is there. He is holding a clipboard. Pustules dot his cheeks. He says he is a census taker.

Maybe it is true, as Father says, that I need to work on compassion. I send the man packing. Closing the door, I think, *Why so angry at a fat man with pustules?* And I am filled with unease.

There is a prickling sensation around my eyebrows, and my eyes feel fat. Two or three minutes later, a light sweat chills my arms and upper lip. I hold my breath. Then, when I think the danger has passed, I bring up a tiny slug of phlegm, about the size of a Tylenol capsule.

They say you always love your own. Well, you can tell them from me, it's a lie. I feel about as much for my phlegm as I would for a scrap of baloney trim. Fold it in a napkin and dispose of it! Though to be honest I do not do that. I touch it. I manipulate it. All right, I lose control, I wring and shunt and crimp and "volunteer" and I even lie down and roll on it.

At first I perform these actions with an ironic air, like a person with free will, who is doing something wrong or absurd for her own reasons. But the feeling comes over me that there is very little difference between doing something ironically and just doing it. So I resolve to stop touching the phlegm. Then I discover that I want to touch the phlegm, very much, and there is nothing ironic about it. Then I fight against it with the feelings of a martyr. Immediately I am bested. I fling myself at the phlegm and indulge myself upon it more violently than ever before.

When I am done I have another little freak. "I'll call you family," I say, "my little kelpie, and I'll sew you a little nightgown with my own two hands. Yeah, *sure* I will."

I take the thing outside and throw it in the Handi Humus.

After this, I cannot stop phlegming. I phlegm for a commercial, an old photograph, a red windbreaker. Only Father has the power to dry me up.

I tell myself that it is time to stop riding the high horse of the tramp who knows her way around phlegm, and get help. So I talk to this girl at work.

"Let me get this straight," she says. "You're trying to have *less* phlegm? I should be so afflicted."

"But some random guy comes to the door? Some, like, clipboard guy? And for him I start phlegming?"

"Well, why not, I mean it's perfectly natural. You just have to stay present with the phlegm and honor the miracle of it. You can't dictate when and where you'll phlegm. That's one thing I've learned. From Mordechai? In my Phlegm Fitness Workshop?"

She gives me a flyer. It says,

EXPLORE PHLEGM PHITNESS WITH MORDECHAI™!

Blocked? Impacted? Abundance limitations? We practice opening to phlegm in a safe setting through Faucet work, releasing negative core constructs that block phlegm expression at the wellspring. More advanced students work with the phlegm directly, practicing guided pastry and personal-imagery curdling, developing a sense of empowerment through hands-on learning of practical phlegm-management techniques. Did you know that just being present with your vents can increase flow?

Go with the Phlow—with Mordechai™!

"Hello, dear persons!"

"Hello, Mordechai!"

"We're all here because we want to get friendly with our phlegm. Let's take a minute to acknowledge that this is a sad moment but also a happy one. How sad that we are holding back our phlegm for whatever reason! At the same time, how natural! How great that we are able to admit that we have a problem and take the plunge of spending a little money to work on the problem with someone like me who while not materialistic has to keep the wolf from the door. How great for me to be honored with the gift of helping people with their phlegm problems.

"Don't worry if the phlegm doesn't come, at first. What matters is that you take the time to sit and open yourself to the possibility of phlegm and accept whatever comes. If it's a thin dribble, great! If it's nothing at all, that's great too! Some of you will get big yields right off the bat and will be feeling pretty pleased with yourselves and others will be looking at you and feeling kind of downcast about their own meager productions. This is natural, but it's not a place to get stuck. This is not about who has the best phlegm. Someone with low yield may have a better relationship to herself and her phlegm than you high-volume folks.

"Now, you may be a little self-conscious and that can dry you right up. Some of you may actually feel like you have gotten worse, not better, in this environment of safety and empowerment and may be saying quietly to yourself, *Hey Mordechai, what gives?* Just know that's perfectly natural and will pass. If nothing comes at first, just fake it. Sometimes playacting will open the floodgates. And if not, there's no harm in learning some techniques to practice later!

"So let's do it, persons. Let's cast the phlegm.

"Pat it around a little, get friendly with it, tell yourself *Okay, this is my phlegm.* Sit back on your haunches and look at it. Good!

"Okay, let's get silly with this, albeit for a serious purpose. Do you know the Country Dance? This is the Bank Robbery. This is the Potato Ricer. Shrimping. Bindling. Franking. The Bamboo Hutch. The Tenderfoot. Good! Good!"

I speak to Mordechai. I tell him about my phlegm fluctuations: molto phlegm here, zip there. We discuss disgust. I tell him about my father and his thumbs. Mordechai thinks it may be a growth experience to yield to my father in this matter. "Give a little, dear person," says Mordechai, rubbing my shoulder. "Lose that legacy of pain!" [See Appendix 4.]

Finally I decide to do the thing with my thumbs. It is indescribably vile. A little involuntary phlegm starts from Father's throat vent. I pretend it isn't there even when it puddles on his bib. I take the afternoon off, meaning I stay in my room and ignore his cries.

I stand at the window. It is more of a mirror than a window. It is so dark outside with the phlegm closing in that I can only see my face.

I see what my face is thinking. It is thinking, *This does not work for me.* I cannot go with the Phlow.

I am surprised to find myself rooting for the fat-bottomed chick. Way to go with that hose! Water that lawn! I feel what she feels when her shoulders sag and she drops the dry hose. There is no point in bothering, we feel together, if she waters the bush today, she might not water it tomorrow or ever again, can she really anticipate in all honesty that she will water the bush every day or even every week, no, and if not, why give the shriveled bush a little water-slash-hope, why not let it die ASAP, so the guilt and regret will be over sooner. *What a sorry-ass*, she is thinking, *I can't even water my damn bush.*

"Ask her to come over," says Father. "And you can rustle us up a little kirsch!"

I go across the street. She takes off when she sees me but she is pretending not to notice me so I figure it will be OK if I pretend not to notice her pretending not to notice me and I follow her up the driveway, watching her behind. Father is right about her keister. It is big, but friendly.

She turns around and sighs. She swipes at her throat and garners a bit of phlegm and holds out her hand politely. I feel Father watching, so I finger it gingerly. I know what she is thinking and I know what to say.

"Look at me, I've got a phlegm blob growing in my humus pile! You think you're weird?"

She gives me the hairy eyeball. "You have what?" She walks away. I remember too late that just because a person is pathetic doesn't mean she can necessarily forgive other people for being pathetic. I should know.

. . .

"May I please speak to Mr. Nimnick?"

"This is no longer the Nimnick number."

I come home from work and see, first, a small pile of monies on the table, where no monies should be. In fact they are in a salad bowl, and look something like a salad no longer crisp. Second, I see a group of miscellaneous persons sitting in what might pass for lotus positions in a semicircle on the floor. Some of them look peaceful, others uneasy. At the focus of the semi-circle sits my father in his chair, flapping his flippers, a drop agleam under his nose.

"What is happening here?" I say. "Can someone explain to me in a nutshell what is going on?"

"Um, maybe Sensei should speak to that?" says a young man with beard all the way down his neck. He is looking at Father. Father says nothing, just nods. He seems to be smiling.

"I'm waiting," I tell them.

A woman in a salmon-colored pantsuit clears her throat. "May we know your name?" she says. Eventually I get out of her that she got the address from the paper. Eventually I find out that Father has used my credit card to put an ad in the paper advertising "Transformative Touch with a Master."

I hand back the money, which is awkward, because some have paid for ten classes with free introductory session, and some for one at full price, and some have not paid at all but just rummaged in the salad bowl a little and these naturally do not want to admit it, and in the end we are forty dollars short, and there is yelling.

I blow up. "Hello, am I in Spooky World? Can someone explain to me how it makes sense that this is happening? Trans-

formative Touch, my fat ass!" I hold the door open. "Get out before I Transformative Touch you where the sun don't shine!" I
throw the money out after and slam the door. There is a lot of
scrabbling, then silence.

I have the phone shut off. There will be no more mysterious
charges on my credit card. There will be no more calls for Sensei, or for Mr. Nimnick. There will be no more calls for anyone.

We watch the neighbor all the time now, hungrily, as if what she
does will decide our own fate. Phlegm broods above the treetops, but the neighbor's red windbreaker still catches the sun
and it is brave if a little pathetic against the gloom.

    We watch with considerable surprise as she unlocks the shed.
We are impressed that she knows where the key is. We are impressed with the familiar way she seizes the heavy padlock and
tugs. But that is nothing compared to how impressed we are
when she comes out pushing a lawnmower ahead of her. I get
a little misty-eyed. It is possible, then: people change. Lawns
can be mowed, in the faith that other days of mowing will follow, or that even if they are only ever mowed once, that mowing has some absolute merit.

    We watch her lay the heavy orange extension cords down the
step. There is no end to the capabilities of this remarkable
woman.

    She mows the entire front lawn, pacing back and forth like a
monk. She mows the grassy hump up the middle of the driveway between the tire tracks. We watch her only slightly
hunched back recede as she heads toward the backyard.

    The motor cuts off.

    We are surprised to see her coming out the front door,

though we shouldn't be, it's perfectly logical that she would have a back door, and—why not, after the show of competence she has already made—that she has had the foresight to unlock it. She is carrying the end of the extension cord and she walks back around the house beside the orange line, which peels up some distance behind her and takes itself with her as she goes. Then she must have plugged it in again, probably in the kitchen, because the motor starts up.

"Now!" says Father. "Go now, and bring her back to us. She is just what we need."

He's right! I cross the lawn in the smell of grass and head up the driveway. The motor stops again.

The small backyard is half mowed. She is lying on her face. I roll her over. Her eyes are open white. How strange the white orbs look in those lids that make the shapes of two wrinkled, sad little mouths.

Of course my phlegm comes [see Appendix 5]. "Weird timing, I know. It isn't you," I explain, and then I notice she is not listening.

The fat-bottomed woman is dead. She ran her lawnmower over the extension cord. The stupid cops said she might have done it on purpose. But as Mrs. Nachtsheim said so rightly, there's no way she would choose to die leaving a dirty litter box.

"She died," I tell Father every morning. Every morning he weeps. Somehow he has gotten it into his head that I am to blame. "You certainly put the kibosh on that romance," he says bitterly. "You certainly have the killer instinct." Lately he refuses to let me wipe his nose. He sits and stares out the window. A guy with yellow hair and black eyebrows has rented the fat-bottomed woman's house. Mrs. Nachtsheim has adopted the cat. The cat gets out of Mrs. Nachtsheim's house every few days and sits on the lawn at the fat-bottomed woman's house. The lawn that is never mowed.

I bite off my thumbs.

Appendix 1

Phlegm and Me: A Primer
B. Ambler, Wesley School Book Company, Chicago, 1897

The stuff of which the phlegm is made is very light and fine, and at first scarcely viscous at all, but as it is plied, folded and fluted, its texture changes. Touch it! Can you feel the difference? It is stickier and more resilient. With Mr. Microscope to help us, we can see wondrous alterations on the molecular level: the round atomies are joining hands with other atomies, and collecting into little strings! Soon, other changes begin to happen. Some of these strings connect to each other at an angle, and when there are three of them, it may happen that the third string connects to the beginning of the first string, making a triangle. Four strings make a square, a diamond, or a trapezoid! How many shapes can you name? Tiny cubes and pyramids are rapidly built and demolished. Then more complicated forms, so many we don't even have names for them all! When you hear the phlegm is "castling," this is what is meant.

Here's where *you* can help. By itself, the phlegm will become a shapeless mound bristling with little points. But by touching and folding the phlegm, you can give it a beautiful form and an

even texture. It may seem bossy and mean to restrict the exuberance of the phlegm, but we have seen how this exuberance
ends up. Messy! The disciplined phlegm is harmonious and ra-
diates well-being. It does not shout, "Look at me!" It is simple
and modest, like good boys and girls. This work can be done
alone, but when two people love each other very much, shaping the phlegm together becomes a wonderful way of express-
ing their cordial feelings.

We do not go to these lengths for a simple greeting, of course.
A standardized series of kneading gestures in a one-two-three
count will suffice. The "We'd better lance that," the "From
where I was sitting it looked out to me" and the "I'm trying to
find my way in dense fog" series are the most widely accepted
today, but others will come into vogue and these will come to
look a little quaint, just as the most common gestures of yester-
year (the "Goosey goosey gander" and "What's this in my
pocket?") seem to us today.

Appendix 2

"Commercial Phlegm: Bane or Boon?"

Llewellyn Turk, American Pastimes *no. 133, May 1961*

Don't be deceived by the packaging. Commercial brands of
phlegm differ only in the dyes and fragrances they add. There
is really only one way to make phlegm. (I exclude of course that
cheap novelty also sometimes called phlegm—though it is
hardly worthy of the name—made of cornstarch, food coloring,
and water, and often adulterated with sequins and canned sen-
timents on slips of colored paper. You've seen it at checkout

stands in supermarkets and gas stations; it reaches its nadir in those garishly colored or, worse, glow-in-the-dark souvenirs peddled at holiday resorts, ball games, beaches, and amusement parks, with their thematic enclosures: mini soccer balls, international flags, and the like.)

Phlegm is milked from naturally high-yield individuals, often illegally, in huge third-world "spit shops" much like factories, where an unnatural and unhealthy level of production is induced by the all-dairy diet, fondling (performed by crack teams of fondlers, often underage), short films, etc. This phlegm is whisked out of the area to ensure that as little imprinting as possible takes place between the parent and the phlegm.

In a holding shed it is spread out in huge shallow tanks and slowly decocted under moonlight, a process that takes some weeks; daytimes it is covered with heavy black tarpaulins to retard evaporation, since the decoction must be slow to allow the phlegm to become completely alienated from the parent psyche. This is a solemn period of separation, introversion, the putting aside of the easy attractions of a world of a thousand and one desires.

Next, the phlegm, thickened but not quickened, is rolled up in big, soft pancakes and shunted down the belt to a forcing chamber, where it is sieved through a series of ever finer screens, the last one of pure silk, after which it has lost whatever accidental form the decoction tanks bestowed on it. Now it is a pure inchoate jelly.

Next comes the "rapport," the phase for which skeptics reserve their strongest criticisms: how can the phlegm come to maturity through the offices of a machine? Be that as it may, the fact remains that after yielding to a vigorous kneading under the paddles, then a delicate spindling and fluting around the fingerlike spools in the agitator, the phlegm is almost indistinguishable from natural phlegm, with the following differences (good or bad, depending on your viewpoint): that it is sanitary, and that it is free of those neurotic formations that often castle spontaneously in the phlegm of even quite normal individuals.

This concludes my summary of the industry. That working conditions must be stringently reviewed and, where necessary, regulated, is obvious. May concerned parties take note! These issues aside, I confidently recommend the use of machined phlegm in all situations where hygiene is of concern, as well as those numerous social situations where the individual is concerned to make a good impression, and his or her own phlegm is not "up to snuff."

Appendix 3

Together in Phlegm: A Couple's Manual
Dr. B. Marcus, Barnum and Brewster, 1989

Phlegm energy, or P, flows along tiny natural capillaries or canals, which form a latent structure within the apparently formless corpus or hunk. By working the phlegm and pressing images through the tiny canals in much the way one works a fugitive elastic through a waistband, the canals become opinionated, and the P energy flows freely toward and through the construction sites. Deformations are caused by P energy balking at tight spots and clogging the canals, making the pinched opinion spritz. Its scattered bits and pieces knit together into a degraded form of imago, or "booger." By applying a little focused nostalgia to kinks and pressure points on the canals, you can release the opinion and set the engine back in motion. Put your whole family behind your movements. Allow your father to rock gently: pushing, pulling. Your mother should be close to, but not touching, the surface; this is called feathering. The imago is never an undifferentiated lump, but is criss-crossed by nostalgic forces. Only you can bring these in harmony.

When a person is in full flood, and the phlegm is cresting and rising high, and her hands are plunged in it to the elbow, possibly alongside those of her "bedroom apprentice" (other terms: *lady* or *gentleman-in-helping, scapemeet, pillow sharecropper*), then it is best not to interfere. The tricky geometries of the castling phlegm, bricking over the imaginary objects held in mind by the parent/custodian, can take a wrong turn, and though the custodian toils on, the edifice is, to use a technical term, cursed. Suffice it to say that an object that is almost necessary is more unnecessary than an object that was never intended to be necessary in the first place, which can acquire a kind of necessity of grace. That this has taken place sometimes escapes the attention of the custodian, who is involved in settling intricate rhythmic tantrums, and can install many images in the phlegm before she realizes, too late, that the whole enterprise has already received the big kayo.

There are many recurring motifs in the myriad forms of couples' phlegm. Notable among these are *approach* (which includes the teasing display of the phlegm vents, "paradise flaunting," and playful splattering and dabbing gestures) and *avoidance* (most famously, cold-cocking: the sudden unsticking of a ball of hardened phlegm, which will take off the small hairs, but also the "kick in the seat of the pants," etc.). Many regional and personal variations are possible and include mixing rice with the phlegm ("extra pulp") for friction, "cuddling," "brooding," etc. But I will ask you to abandon these or any other tricks you feel you have mastered. It is exactly this feeling of "mastery" that gets in the way of direct experience.

Touch the phlegm. Feel yourself one with the phlegm. What do you, the phlegm, want to express? As you open yourself to the phlegm's desire, your fingers may wish to make certain movements. Yield to these impulses, but if you find yourself falling into a familiar pattern, slow down. Do not name the pattern to yourself. Stay with the phlegm. Let it teach you what it wants to become. Perhaps it does want you to perform the Chrysanthemum or the beautiful old steps of the Invitation. If so, it will show you. You will discover them all over again, and they will be yours, and not a rote recital of a classic. Avoid influence as well. Your friends may call you chic, but are you sure you will be happy tomorrow with the giant peonies of today?

Except to those bowed by the winds of fashion, it does not really matter what form you attempt to impose on the phlegm. The particular form is a sort of pretext, though a necessary one, for it is only through our attention and toil that the phlegm can mature. This is not to say that the particular form does not matter, that it is just an envelope, because phlegm never *is* until it *is something*, so however arbitrary the process of composition, the phlegm endows the result with its own dignity, and makes even a hackneyed idea into a special case.

I should like to close this chapter with a quote from an anonymous nineteenth-century author. I hope you, too, will take inspiration from its freshness, its naïveté, its freedom from the proscriptions and prescriptions of the larger world.

"And then was born in me the desire to try my hand upon the phlegm, and see what I might shape, and its substance seemed very comely and lustrous to me, and its touch was as a liniment to my hands, and it seemed pleased to feel my touch, like an affectionate cat, thrusting its back strongly against the caress. And it was given to me then to make many beautiful forms, some of which arose and melted away as quickly as the clouds that gather and disperse without distress to the sky or the earth, but only delight to the eyes, and other forms were more lasting, and as I manipulated them, and returned to them again and again in my delight to fondle them, and at times threw my whole weight against them in proud trial of their strength, they became ever more brazen and hard, and among these forms were several sheep, a complicated tower or turret, and a fascinating hole."

Appendix 4

Coming to Phlegm: Women Talk About Their First Flow
Eds. Wilson and Wilson, Spindrift Press, 1992
    "Jane"

As a kid, I had the usual romantic notions about phlegm, I played pat-a-cake and practiced molding on mud and clay. One by one the other kids around me got theirs. One memorable day, seven kids got their first phlegm in the same recess period (it often happens, I found out later, that friends trigger one another—but at the time it seemed like a sign, as did my own omission). I stayed dry.

The happiness of phlegm eluded me despite my most earnest efforts. No man would touch me. I had zero self-esteem. I was in the depths of despair. One day, I caught sight of myself in the mirror. I hardly recognized myself! My ceaseless straining to produce phlegm had made my eyes cold and my lips thin and pursed. I groaned: "I give up! I will try to live a decent life, though I am that saddest of creatures—a dry woman!"

And then my phlegm broke. It was so simple, I laughed out loud. I was still here, the world still there, but somehow I was able to extend this in-me-ness into that out-there-ness. I began to mold my phlegm. I cannot describe the joy I felt. The molding, I saw, was a kind of clarifying and articulating of what was already there, but it was at the same time an act of pure invention and discovery, in which I became myself in an impossibly prolonged moment of transformation, while not ceasing to be what I already was and had always been, and this whole event was, as I understood, a demonstration (in which the phlegm was equally instructional aid, teacher, and student) of the beautiful truth that . . .

Appendix 5

The Viscid Enigma: Phlegm
Leslie Stace, PhD, Cordolu University Press, 2001

That there has always been something eerie about phlegm, something that stirs man's dark imaginings, can be seen by examining the concordance of myths. Wizards who create servants or concubines out of their own phlegm are sure to be driven to madness and death by their creations; fairies who steal mortal children often replace them with an identical creature made all of phlegm; a dead woman's face will appear in her murderer's phlegm during congress with his new lover.

Graves that flow with phlegm are a staple of folk storytelling around the world, but were long considered no more than fantasies by men of science. Imagine the stir it caused when in 1970 a Canadian researcher proved (in the rather sensationally titled *The Extraordinary Case of the Dead Mr. Fleming*) that some bodies do continue phlegm production—indeed, step it up—for some days after all other bodily functions have ceased. Bodies have been disinterred whose coffins are quite full of phlegm, such that the deceased is found embedded in a sort of sticky amber, like a prehistoric gnat. We may perhaps find in this phenomenon of extended postmortem phlegm production the factual basis for the accounts of those saints (technically known as Myroblites) whose relics exude "balm and aromatic ichors." ("Aromatic" is devout embroidery, we may be sure.)

Even in modern times, an aura of mystery surrounds these bodies lapped in phlegm. *The Extraordinary Case* drily proposes that the semiautonomous phlegm engines are always primed, even in the dry old age of the driest specimen of humankind, and that when the body relaxes its guard—and death may be seen as a kind of absolute relaxation—the phlegm backlog will out. But even our laconic French-Canadian friend waxes lyrical in his concluding remarks. "What do these bodies teach us?" he queries. "Are they in some sense still alive? Are they striving, in their wordless, affecting way, to express their tenderness and forgiveness to the living?"

HAIR

Her girlfriend left but she found she was not alone in the house. "Let me speak," said the hair. She recognized it as one of her own. She had thought it was gone forever, but forever does not always last very long.

"I am amazed to see a hair stand alone, upright in the air," she said. "So speak."

The hair had a brassy light in its shaft. It stood and shone and swayed, and a wave ran up it and down and the frequency of the wave was such that a clear note was laid upon the air, and so the hair began to sing, and it sang these words: "Many a little makes a mickle, once bitten twice shy, time and tide wait for no man, a penny saved is a penny earned."

She assented to everything the hair said, and felt in her heart that the hair was right, and furthermore he cut a gallant figure, did slim, insinuating Mr. Hair. Would she step out with him? Why, yes.

At the appointed hour the hair came back and it brought friends. Together they swayed and arched like a wave. Light struck deep into the glassy swells. One hair curled and bounced like spindrift above the rest.

"Trust no man, though he be your brother," sang the hair, "who has hair one color, and beard another. Loose lips sink ships. Out of sight, out of mind." She held out her hands, and the hair coiled around her wrists once, twice, many times. Then it towed her into the wave.

But when she was alone again, her heart changed, and the sight of her own hair on her shoulders filled her with loathing, and so she took clippers in hand and gave herself a buzz cut. All the hairs rose up upon the kitchen floor and danced around her feet, and then one by one they threaded themselves through the keyhole and were gone.

Now she entered into a time of trial. If she bent over a nosegay in a glass, a hair whipped itself many times around her nose and tweaked it. A hair lay coiled in every soupspoon she brought to her lips. She loathed lawns and would not picnic, because the hairs hidden among the grass blades bent over the cloth and nodded mockingly at her.

Now when she walked down the street the children shouted after her: "Mistress Mary quite contrary how does your garden fare? With silver hairs and golden hairs and hairy hairy hairy hair!"

At the museum she saw the hair in a Hogarth; it was disguised as a line, but she found it out, because she marked how sinuous and solitary it was, and that it was not content to stay coiled in the skirt of a bawd, but slung itself around a drunkard's throat, humped along the back of a cur snarling at a rat, and arched from a lad's trousers to the puddle on the ground. "There's my hair," she said. "I would know it anywhere." And she did: she knew it on the backseat of a car, recumbent between floorboards, on the shoulder of a gentleman's tweed overcoat, in the gutter of a book open to a page on which a careful reader would find the word *lies* written six times over, on a bus, in a restaurant, in a video store, at a lecture, at a political rally.

She took a walk in the park. She mounted a small rise, and the sun struck through the trees at her, and blinded her as she advanced. She shaded her eyes and saw a blazing shield. Between two trees, across the path, hung a spider's web as big as a garden gate. It was almost complete; a shining spider stepped, conjured the silk from its abdomen, stretched the line, dipped, rose, and let it snap into place. But it was not silk, no, the spider was spinning a web of hair. She ran from the horrible thing.

When she got home, she started a letter to her girlfriend. An old-fashioned letter, on paper. She signed her name at the bottom. But when she lifted her pen, she pulled her signature straight. Then all her words unraveled. The letters lost their loops and slithered right off the page. She had written a letter to her lover. Oh, what had the letter said?

The hair is a subtle spirit, and noose to our passions. It counsels policy, silence, and circumspection, and its songs incite no candid lunge to pen or gun, but the slow asphyxiation of deceit. In its coils the very breath studies cunning. Once broken, the body rises lightly and easily to the lie, and if you ever slip, the hair will knot around your neck, and hoist you up.

SLEEP

Sleep is falling. The crumbs run in drifts down the street, collect in the gutters.

Sleep falls every day at noon here, with soothing regularity. Sometimes it melts on the way down, and falls as golden rain, or in cold weather, golden sleet, but mostly our siesta is warm and dry. The occasional sleepstorm is cozy and harmless: a war waged with croutons and dinner rolls. Once, years ago, when the children were young, we woke to find we were slept in: I opened the front door and the living room filled with gold. We had a sleepball fight around the sofa, which my wife won—she was always fierce in defense of her own. The drifts blew away by evening, but our house was gilded until the next rain, and the shrubs were like torches!

Where we live, the skies are heavy with sleep. Sometimes high-flying jets come down encrusted with it, like bees dusted with pollen. Fielded by Midas and thrown home, how beautiful these shining apparitions are. They roll unsteadily to a stop, transformed into fairy-tale coaches. A crack opens, a patch of golden coral swings aside, stairs descend, and then the baffled pilot emerges like a new Aphrodite from a peculiar Edenic shell.

Permanent banks and shoals of sleep drowse above us. They can be thick enough, it is whispered, to slow a plane to a standstill and hold it fast above the earth. Some planes disappear and are never found. Some fall to earth, but no human remains are discovered in the wreckage. Many years ago, a pilot landed a plane alone, and insisted forever after that everyone else got out *above*, forced open the emergency exits in mid-flight and stepped out into a landscape of gilt towers and archways.

Sleep sometimes coagulates in the shapes of animals: bruin and bunny are the most common, though I have seen sheep and cows as well. These form naturally, like snowflakes. Under favorable conditions these sleep-sheep "stalk the earth," the colloquial term for wafting or "mere wafting," as O'Sullivan pointedly calls it, eschewing what he calls the "credulous jargon of simpletons and charlatans." He is practically alone in his refusal to see familiar forms in sleep, of course. Animalcules take shape in every substance known to us; it is a tendency written into the very structure of matter, a statistically significant swerve toward animaloid structures, especially cute ones. The universe, we now know, is far from that chill mechanical model so unaccountably adored by physicists past. The world that gave rise to feathers, pill bugs, cookies, and whales is silly, showy, comfy. Above all, it is kind.

O'Sullivan and his humorless cronies are just the latest incarnation of our abstemious church fathers, who held it a sin to sink into the friendly pillowing of sleep, in which every living thing delights. Sleep, they taught, is the dross of souls rejected by God, who chews us up en masse, strains the juices through his baleen, and spits out the crud. "The damned will stay in hell as broth and yeast," says Luther. Sleep is that broth, that yeast.

Of course, sleep is literally both broth (add water) and yeast: a few grains of it scattered over warm, honey-fattened water will bewitch bread into a fantasia of dough turrets, minarets, grottos, candelabras, and credenzas, now sadly out of culinary fashion, but still traditional at Sleepmastide. Its flavor is unremarkable, though children love it, but I find it has a mild intoxicating effect, albeit short-lived. The taste is reminiscent of cardamom, with an incongruous hint of spearmint. A few grains on the tongue will calm a fretful baby; cooked up and injected, its effects are stronger but still mellow, hence its reputation as a drug for hippies and beginners, though it is probably more frequently taken by users of all descriptions than this reputation would suggest.

Exotic varieties of sleep, named for the region in which they're gathered, are popularly believed to have special qualities, though scientists say there is no significant difference between these and our domestic sleep. My private investigations (the wayward probings of a curious mind) have brought me to the same conclusion. These rare strains of sleep are some countries' biggest cash crop, so their governments turn a blind eye to the traffic, and are not very hospitable to foreign scientists who want to test on-site the exaggerated claims that circulate about the properties of the sleep when fresh.

There are gnostic teachings of another sleep, the opposite in every respect of our sunny everyday sleep. One reads of a dark, greasy, subterranean sleep, which seeps out of solid rock and hardens into strange fungal forms, and plugs underground rivers with a glassy but flexible mass that can be reliquefied by one blow of a pickax. Miners have staggered out of shafts and told tales of slow-motion tsunamis of sour treacle. Do not sample this sleep, they say; it will spoil your appetite for every other thing. Nevertheless, I cannot help wishing that someday I will be given a chance to taste it. I love sleep, I confess, and as I watch the grains fall slowly outside the window, I think how lucky we are. Into our difficult lives this surplus falls. This gift.

I have not mentioned the greatest consolation sleep grants us. At the proper time and with the proper ceremonies, you may make yourself a substitute out of sleep. How to do it must be writ in our genes. I watched my children miming it in sandboxes; like birds building nests, they needed no tutors. You may fail at every other endeavor, but you will not fail at this one. Even the clumsiest become deft and knowing as they pat and roll the golden column, persuading it into human form.

This substitute or scapegoat is legally empowered to act as a person in your stead. Your substitute can vote for you, take a test or a beating, deliver a public speech, perform the marital duties, or commit suicide for you. Politicians are all substitutes, as are firemen, astronauts, and most people forced to make public apologies, but substitutes are often made for sadder, more personal reasons. I have watched friends grow ever more restless and unhappy, until one day the complaining stops, and I know they have gone to start a new life and left this diplomat behind. We say they are "dreaming." I am happy for them in their bright new world.

My children are already dreaming. So young! At their age I kept telling myself, *A better time will come. I can endure this moment.* And when the next moment came, I found I could endure that one too, and so on, to this day. But I don't think less of them for making their escape. We are all waiting for our chance. Out of care and duty leaps the shocking blossom of the new: vibrant, imperious, reeking of pollen. It is a subpoena, a lure, a gauntlet. If we are honest and brave we have little choice: we kick over our happy home and go. We step out of the airplane onto a golden cloud.

It is a terrible thing when it is the substitute that is sent to find a new life, a sign that a person yearns for change but cannot imagine creating it herself. The irony is that her failure of imagination marks her proxy, too. When you see someone creeping through life, as if everything in the world were new, yes, but in its newness an assault, she is sure to be one of these.

An action is in the works to protect the rights of substitutes. It is bound to fail, because the substitutes themselves show no interest in it; the meetings of the Substitutes' Union are all attended by solicitous originals who—in an odd reversal—are empowered to vote for their substitutes! These good-hearted citizens betray a basic confusion about the existential condition of the substitutes. If scapegoats feel pain, it is only the delegated pain of their originals.

Use your substitute well: you will not get another. If you use it too early—to feign a teen suicide, maybe, or escape the school bully—you must live out your own life from then on, and that is a hard, lonely prospect. People who use their substitutes frivolously find that they have given all their frivolity away, and are compelled to be serious characters from then on, while their substitute dutifully practices dissolution.

Eventually, of course, the substitute has suffered enough knocks that it no longer looks quite human. Dents alter the form little by little; scratches expose the waxy interior.

It is the originals' responsibility to lay their substitutes to rest when this time comes, but not surprisingly, they often fail to take this in hand. (Those battered pawns we've all seen staggering around are a civic disgrace.) When the original is ill or badly hurt, on the other hand, the substitute's pupils turn white, while if the original should die, the substitute falls in its tracks and turns to sleep again, sifting out of the sleeves and collar. This can be a brutal shock to family members who did not know their loved one was a substitute.

If an enterprising person is standing by, this sleep can be patted together again; it is the only time a person can make a second substitute. These secondary substitutes, lit as it were on the embers of the one before, have certain specific defects that do not vary: they cannot enunciate the consonants d or t, they cannot create nested sentence structures, they are color-blind, and they have recurring nightmares of spiral forms and infinitely mounting abstract quantities.

No substitutes can have children, in the usual run of things, although they make kind, responsible parents. A substitute wife can become "pregnant" and in due course deliver a waxy figurine, but this baby will not move or cry, since it has no original and is not a true substitute.

There is a mystical tradition that if two substitutes fall in love (true love must be specified, for many marriages are made up of a pair of substitutes, in fact nothing is more common), their child has a fifty-fifty chance of being an original. If such a child is born, and reality thus springs from the loins of artifice, then all people will fall to their knees before it. It will be the living god, and this can be proved by conjuring it to make a substitute for itself. The sleep will fall apart in the child's hands: the real Original can have no substitutes.

Last night I lay awake, and in one of the thousand insomniac hours before dawn I switched on a lamp. A fine scar on my wife's eyelid caught the light and gleamed like a gold thread. I turned back the sheets, I examined her entire body, and I found incontrovertible proof. My wife is a substitute. As I got out of bed, she mumbled something and reached for me. I touched her hand and saw her smile into the pillow.

I am not shocked. Is that dreadful? She could not endure the demands of our love and she left. I understand this as I have understood other surprises she has given me in the past. I feel lonely, and yet in a curious sense there is something right about this. I have spent my life in adoration of sleep. I may have loved it better—more carefully, more knowledgeably—than I've loved the people in my life. Its beauty, its mystery. The evidence it bears of a universe capable of mercy. Now when I say I love sleep, I can also say I love nothing else. Everything I love is made of it.

The sleep is falling steadily. I could go out and gather it. I could pat it together. My hands would know what to do. I used to be a pilot, did I mention that? I would like to make one more flight. This time I would not let my chance go by.

I could leave my life. I could change completely. Is it time?

SANGUINE

BLOOD

It wasn't steady work, no, no more than once a month, and then it was terrible hard work for a few days. But the pay was good. I can't complain. It was a sight better than singing "Mother, Is the Battle Over?" at the crossroads and plying my broom before the gentlemen and ladies—I was always more clever than pretty, and made less for all my winking and scraping than the other girls did just sitting there. I thank my stars for the night I fell in behind the blood wagon; I made myself such a pestilential bother with asking questions that Scratch Jill finally took me on as apprentice and I never missed a period the next twenty year. I was a devil for working. I worked on the docks in between, though I needn't have and some like me didn't, but just lazed around until the monthly came again.

My informant is a hale woman in her forties, robust, with a head of ginger hair untidily seamed with white. She wears a gentle-man's tweed coat with bone buttons over her simple gown of green stuff, and sports a man's hat rather than a bonnet. The effect is not without dignity, for she carries herself well, and her

*unconventional costume seems to be a matter of preference
rather than necessity, as her income is adequate to her needs.
She is unmarried, and counts herself lucky to have been employed as a swabber in the now obsolete blood pipes. The city
pensioned her at an early age when it modernized the drainage
system, but she still takes odd jobs. She keeps to herself. Her life
has not always been so sedate, but now she prides herself on
keeping up her home, which while small is neat and well-
appointed. Only over a pint does she relax and allow herself to
expand about the old times.*

*She has stopped her account and now stares for long mo-
ments into the yeasty depths of her pint glass. Who knows what
she sees there? I have no doubt that her life has been hard, but
only at such moments does her manner reveal any discontent. It
is quickly shaken off, however, and her narrative is picked up
again.*

Out in the country they let it come up wherever it pleases. Well,
they can't stop it, can they? My sister lives in Kent. Once a
month the blood wells up in the cow prints. Perfect little cups
of it, she says they are, and make a pretty trail through the
cowslips. Blood runs down the bark of trees, why I don't know,
maybe the roots drink it in below, and it comes out above. It
fills the ruts and runs between the cabbages. Why make a fuss
about it, my sister wants to know. It helps the plants grow, is
what they say, and does no harm to animals either, and even
humans will take a nip on the sly, for the power it is said to
have to bring true dreams of love and put a powerful charm of
attraction on the drinker.

Whether it brings love to them as drinks it I don't know. It
brought love to me, but I was soaked in it from top to toe every

month for twenty year. But Sally is gone now, and I don't care to speak of her.

I was a blood-lark, yes, that's what they called us back then. We wasn't pretty, we was a sight to strike fear into the hearts of men, or women, and I won't say we didn't take some pleasure in that, rollicking down the street gin-drunk (they always allowed us a tipple on the job to keep our spirits up; it was hard work, and dirty) heading home at five in the morning in our red coats dripping for all we had squeezed them out into the cart. And singing one of our carols, which were that tuneful, I still find myself humming them, though not one woman in a hundred could join in, for they're forgotten now. But I won't sing one, and you oughtn't to ask. The words would bring up your green bile, if you wasn't used to them, most people being able to handle blood on its own, or lewdness, but the combination being a mite strong for them. Now it's not such a jolly profession, now they do things proper and they've got the machines.

Oh, I wouldn't go back to the old ways, I'm not saying that, just that we had good times and we was always helpful with one another, and indeed we had to be, stuck up to our necks or our ankles depending on which way about we went in, mucking out the blood by main strength if we was in a hurry, or for those as took life more sanguine, just lying and soaking it up slow in our napkin coats. Sanitaries, they called them, but I don't know that they were all that sanitary. Of course, they called them that to have a way to refer to them with gentlefolk, like the ladies what took such an interest in our little ones, the tiddlers we employed back then to swab out the smallest holes. Tiddlers? Children, I mean. Sent them up into the tight spots with cotton balls clenched in their teeth, we did, and pinched their toes if they were slow about it, but we was gentle with them, if they didn't argue too much, and they mostly didn't, you see, because they knew we would drop them in the drink if they did, and they were scared of the blood.

That wears off. Blood is blood, for us as have to wade in it and make our living off it, and it's bonny stuff once you get over being squeamish. There's no place for squeamish girls, not in our trade; we threw 'em right in the catch, heels over head, and had a good laugh, too, while they pulled themselves out, for there isn't a dimity handkerchief in the world what could mop up that mess. Bonny? Yes, that's what I said. Isn't it the very soul of red?

I suppose there was a time the blood came up in the city same as everywhere else. But I don't know when that was. As far back at least as the Romans they was devising ways to keep it away from the city, let it flow as strong as it likes elsewhere. They had lead pipes, and aqueducts, and they sank wells and flushed the gutters with buckets of water and these methods didn't change much for oh, hundreds on hundreds of years, and I suppose they worked well enough, but people was always trying to come up with new ways to draw off the blood and send it somewhere else, the men being most especially particular about it, not having the feel for the blood that women do, and not thinking it right to turn the faucet once a month or work the pump and it runs red, or winch the bucket up and find it brimming with blood. And it's true enough that it is not the stuff to be washing the fine linens in nor to water a delicate wine, though as it only comes once monthly I'd not bother about it if it was up to me.

So here in England they dug and tunneled under London and fashioned the wells and the catches and what all, what were the wonder of the modern world and ain't matched even yet in poorer countries. All the little veins collected the blood and ran it down into the catches and that more or less kept it from rising up in the streets like it used to do, though you could still see beads of blood in city gardens in the morning, for you can't keep the earth from doing what the earth must, and I for one don't want to. Yes, it still come up and pinked the water from the tap and beaded between bricks and cobblestones and trickled down gutters, but most of it was caught in the big catches the little veins run into.

They couldn't just leave it there. Oh, no. Blood does scab, don't it, though the monthly scabs blessedly slow, without which fact we would be scab pickers not swabbers, and I for one thank my stars. Still, if they left it puddling there in the catch, even granted they flush the streets and the buildings and let the runoff go in the catch and water it thin, in a month's time the catch would be one solid scab, like in the scab mines out east, but no use to anyone without a thousand years go by to press it hard and turn it to carbuncles, and meanwhile a more notable problem is the blood next time has no place to run to, all the catches being clogged.

I explain all this because I don't know if you know it, and one day all this knowledge will be gone along with us who done the work. Already Little Tam is dead, and Camilla the C**t, and Red Rose, and Singsong Sally—we called her that, sir, because my Sal was always singing, down in the pipes, and an eerie sound it was to have float up from a hell red hole. And I hear Long Arm Lunnie is only just hanging on, and raving about the catches and the swabs and the napkins, and only a few of us able to know what she's talking about, and she younger than me; and all the little blood-larks who came on after me and who I helped to train and pricked their heels to send 'em into the pipes when they was reluctant, they're all grown women now with little ones of their own and don't want to remember what they done before.

What did they do? Well, isn't it obvious? Someone had to go down and clean out all that blood. In some parts of town you can still see the hatches, and I believe there's unfortunate folk now living in some of the catches they overlooked when they went around walling 'em up. The city called them manholes, same as the other kind, but we right off renamed them lady-holes, that being the cleanest version of the name I can report to you, sir, and that was because we was almost all women who did the work, women being small-boned and, as I said, less in-clined to get funny about the blood, but going about the work practical and easy with one another.

We marched off to work whenever we got called, though most of us could sniff out when a period was coming after just a few months on the job, we had such a feel for it. How did we tell? It's hard to say, we just knew, that's all; everyone got a lit-tle queerish right before, and especially when it was late com-ing, then all at once the whole city relaxed, and that's when we got out our poles and our climbing boots. They never called us out before dark, they had some idea that nobody was to know when it was bleeding, that it would upset people of refinement. Whether that was true or not, we never made much secret of it and went to work singing blood carols like I said, and pass the gin, because we was happy to see each other again and happy to be working, the money often running thin enough by the time the next period came. Sometimes we hitched a ride in the swaddling cart, sunk in the mounds of stained batting.

The cart would stop at the particular ladyhole for which we

was responsible. The lads who stayed above to handle the batting started setting up the big reel, and we patted the horse and some of us patted the lads and down we went like ants into the ground. All over the city at the same time teams like ours was going down the ladyholes single file, hand over hand down the big staples stuck in the walls, with our lanterns fixed to our chests or hats to leave us both hands for climbing. In the circle of sky above, sometimes we could see the cart horse looking down if he came close enough to the fence we put up to keep the people coming late out of the pubs from joining us too sudden.

The first whiff of the blood smell always struck hard, but after that we didn't notice it, it was not a bad smell anyhow, but strong and natural, like horses or a good clean pond with plenty of crawlies living in it. It's foul work, you'll be thinking. Yes. But I say, and others will say the same, that going down that hole, I felt my spirit rise to see the cardinal color on the bricks all around, in the wavery light, and the snowy coats swaying with the climbing, but made so stiff by the quilting they stayed almost the perfect shape of bells, and Sally already tuning up, so powerful a sound in the well, you looked everywhere else first to see who was singing before you came to her mouth moving, and then you was amazed to see the tiny figure who put it out.

There was always a fearful moment when the cozy, lit-up chimney bellied out below into the dark of the catch and we had to take our leave of the staples for the rope ladder. But once we got down far enough that our lights darted around the dome, it was a beautiful sight and enlarged the soul like a cathedral, and that helped with the dizziness.

I mentioned how my Sal was not much in the size depart-
ment. In fact we was all tiny; us grown women were not much
bigger than the tiddlers in training. There was even one proper
dwarf among us, Big Bess we called her, because she was
stocky, though no more than three foot tall. We had to be little
to fit up the pipes. True, anyone agile enough to climb down
could stand watch over the batting coming down, though you
had to be monstrous fit to run up every other minute to pick it
off any snags in the wall. Our own ladyhole had a slight sideways jag, barely enough to notice when you was climbing, but
the tampon always stuck there. If we couldn't worry it loose, we
drew lots for who was going to catch on to the end and hang
there like a clock weight until the batting tore off the snag, and
tampon and swabber both splashed into the catch. There was
no particular danger, sir, for we had ropes and planks all strung
over and around the pool and we could spider about on them
quicker than some folk on solid ground.

That's where the bigger girls stayed, working the batting.
The rest of us was for the pipes what fed into the catch from all
directions, but we always stopped a moment to take in the sight
of the white batting twisting and flinching as it come down from
the hole in the dome. When the batting hit the silky surface red
lights would ripple up the walls as good as a show. That minute,
the cotton wicked up the blood a good five foot. After that the
batting come down steady and slow without too much snagging.
By the end of the night's work, the pool would be gone, and the
whole length of the batting would be lying in fat red swags on
the bottom of the catch, with just the towrope hanging loose
from above and rapping on the sides of the chimney. Then we'd
help the lads reel it up into the cart, which was painted with

pitch so it was mostly proof against leakage, with a few of us staying below to mop the catch clean. Then the next night we had the whole thing to do over, and so on until the period was up.

But I haven't told how we went up the pipes. No, we did no swimming, unless we took an unlucky step on the catwalks and upended into the pool. Only a trickle came from each pipe, so negligible a trickle you wouldn't think the catch would ever fill up off it, but for it came so steady. Up we went in all directions, like ferrets after a rat, in our swaddling suits, prodding the tiddlers ahead of us if we was in an area what had a lot of tiny finicking veins to it, because a finger in the dike is one thing, but you can maneuver better if you can fit your whole fist in there.

The pipes were angled and slippery, but our suits soaked up the blood where they pressed against the walls, and we learned the way of pressing out our elbows against the walls while we brought our knees up, and our knees while we reached up ahead for a handhold. The rubbing of our shoulders and knees did most of the work of cleaning the big arteries, but when we got to the little, crooked bits, what was even too tight for the tiddlers, we got out the swabs and the tampers and the wires with bows of batting tied at the end, and we cleaned all the pokeholes. We lay snug as grubs under the city rubbing all its secret passages clean, working in the dark because we knew where the blood was just by the sticky feel of it and the smell. It wasn't lonely work because the tunnels was like the tubes of a big ear and we could halloo to one another, and more than once someone got in trouble for a whisper or another sound, and that was the time Sally and I had our first fight due to jeal-

ousy, which was before we ever got together, and we took it as
a sign of our being destined, after which we moved in together
and could not be parted.

*My informant is looking into her glass again. I replace it with a
full one.*

Thank you, sir. Yes, I think that's covered it, how we used to do
the job, and I'd like it to be known that we was hardworking,
and clean when at home, cleaner than many as work above in
a fine office. But times move on, and the little bit of blood that
still seeped up to stain the mayor's white gloves on an opera
evening was terrible irksome to him, and so the people what
think things up thought up a better way to keep the blood out
of London, and that was when they modernized, with pumps,
and hydraulics, and deep drilling, and sandbags, and machines
that crawled along pissing gluey stuff, and macadam and such,
so the earth was plugged tight and the city was like a potted
plant, only wet from the top. They put the cart horses to hauling garbage and they let all the swabbers go with a pension,
though there was some funny business which all the girls were
talking about for months about how we only worked part-time,
and our days off counted against our pay like too much sick
leave, which was only what we might have expected from them,
who was reluctant enough to pay us even when they needed us,
but I didn't pay too much attention to it, because my Sal was
sick and I couldn't have left her anyway.

　　Then when she died, my heart smote me if I even glanced at
the ladyholes, and I could not have gone back down there for
any money, and I didn't care if I found other work or not, because I took no joy in anything. I wasn't even curious about the

new machines, and only gradually took note of how clean the streets were, a professional interest, you might call it. Our gang hung together though they found other work; what we had done was a bond, but I kept to myself after Sally died and after a while the girls stopped calling me over to their table, and then I changed pubs and I didn't see them anymore.

We finish our drinks, and take leave of each other.

That should have been the last I saw of her, but for a curious incident some eleven months later, when London town, which had forgotten its swabbers, suddenly found itself in extraordinary need of them. I was able to apprise the mayor that there yet existed (though its ranks were diminished) a class of skilled workers qualified above all others to deliver the city from its distress—if they wanted to. I was able to communicate his need, through my informant, to the remaining swabbers, and with their permission, to broker a generous arrangement for their remuneration. I might indeed have asked any amount, since no one else could do the job which was by then most pressing, but my impromptu clients insisted they wanted their fair pay only—plus a little over, to compensate for the paltry pensions they had received. When I next saw my informant, I had the pleasure of presenting her with a very large check. In return, I begged to hear her account of the affair.

He was a fool! And there's no fool like a proud fool, and that's what he was, a little turkey-cock in high heels. I laughed when I heard he wanted to build the tallest building in London. I'll cast a shadow over Big Ben in the morning, says Mr. Strick, and the dome of St. Paul's in the evening. Never mind that isn't a practicality for geographical reasons. I warrant he had a coven of lawyers working to find a loophole in the laws of nature and believed up to the last minute he would have his way. But build he would, in any event, and let the shadows fall where they might (in the end I think they fell on a rookery, which is where they usually do fall, if truth be told). Such a building he raised, tall and ugly, with no furbelows for the pigeons to perch on. Such a high building must have strong foundations. Deep foundations. I saw the pit—infernal! It struck everyone that way, even me what has spent two decades in the belly of the earth. It was arrogant to dig so low, just as it was arrogant to build so high, neither was really needful—nor lawful, I suppose, though he had money enough to pay the fines. When you're that rich the mayor thanks you for breaking the law!

I won't say I knew it would happen, but the building sat uneasy in my sight. I was on a knife edge anyway, for the monthly was late, and though nowadays I saw not a drop of blood from January through December I still felt when it was coming. My stomach was poorly and it made me come over strange to lean back and look up at the building. Everyone admitted it was indeed very high. All the papers said so. There was a ribbon across the door, which was cut by the little man with the pocketbook, and all his lawyers applauded. The mayor was there, waving. He and Mr. Strick went inside and waved from the big windows and everyone laughed and cheered as if they had done something clever. Then everyone went home.

That night the blood came. I sat up awake in my bed and I knew it was a heavy flow. I heard the tap dripping in the kitchen and I took it in my head that it was blood that was dripping from the tap. I got up to see but the water was clear. So I went back to bed and slept like a baby.

In the morning I heard a hubbub outside but I didn't bother

to ask as there is always a hubbub about something or other. So it wasn't until Big Bess knocked on my door that afternoon with a shine in her eye that I heard. I threw on a coat and clapped a cap on my head and made straight for the Strick building. I had to elbow my way through the crowd once we got in a few blocks of it, Big Bess coming along behind me holding my coattail. We could see plain enough that it was true even before we got to the square it looked over. Mr. Strick had dug too deep and struck through the protection; he had punched a hole right through the flowerpot, sir, into the living earth. And now his building was filling up with blood.

It was a beautiful sight to me, the windows solid red near up to the second floor. The glass of the windows bulged from the press of it. For most of the people there, though, it was a fearful thing. These were city folk, remember, many of them no better acquainted with mother earth than with the man in the moon, and would laugh you down for proposing that an egg comes from the hindquarters of a hen. They don't know blood for the natural thing it is, and I heard mutterings that there was something devilish in the whole business, that if it was not some villainous plan of Mr. Strick's then it was his punishment. Which was true enough, in its way.

The blood lapped at the ceiling of the first floor and it was looking for the way to the second. I had no doubt it would find it. It was rising in the tower like mercury in a glass, and there were many stories to go, and the heaviest flow would come tomorrow. For the first time in years I felt like talking. "Come for a pint, Big Bess," says I, and off we went to a pub.

That was where you found me, sir, some hours later, and perhaps slightly the worse for wear, for I believe I was singing one of the old carols, with Big Bess roaring along, and I must have been in my cups to do that. So I ask your pardon if I was too hearty with you.

At first I was none too sure I wanted the job. It struck me as both pleasing and just that Mr. Strick had himself a towering monument to something even bigger than his opinion of himself: the fat old unstoppable earth. But when it was pointed out to me that with a week to go before the flow died down, the tower couldn't contain all of it, even if the windows held, which was unlikely, I changed my views, because that much blood would drown the whole neighborhood, while Mr. Strick though humiliated would be high and dry, and that was no kind of justice. And maybe it pleased me to be needed again.

Without Bess I couldn't have found the others. But Bess is a natural meddler. Let a stranger come into her pub, she will know his business and give him three pieces of good advice how to do it better before she is through shaking his hand. That's how she is. So she knew where everyone was, swabbers and tiddlers, or knew someone who knew.

You know it very well, for you came along with us, but I'll tell it for the sake of the story, how we went all over town in a hired hansom, very grand for the likes of me, tramping up stairs and knocking on doors and sticking our heads into pubs, and it would have made me come over philosophical if we had not been so busy, to see so many familiar faces, but all carrying more of a burden. I would have liked to fetch the old cart horses, too, who were so steady, and knew their job, and didn't spook at the smell of blood, but they was old and spavined now if they still lived. I don't know how long a horse lives, but they was not young horses even back in the old days. So Bess dug up a motley team of horses from all walks of life. Some was in the

grocery business, some in laundry, some in hauling, and one
was a glossy show horse whose owner owed Bess a favor.

Bess found a failed hospital-linen supplier and by linen I
mean the cheapest cotton sheets, a warehouse full, what were
suffering from the damp and apparently much admired by rats
and cats for their absorbent qualities. The smell on them might
inspire a consumptive to rise from his deathbed and seek more
congenial quarters in the gutter. But they suited our purposes
well enough and the manufacturer, a shiny little red-faced
man, got even redder and shinier, and had to blow his nose on
a sheet. That was nearer than I would have liked to bring my
organ of smell to one of them, but he wanted to show his gratitude.

We loaded the moldy sheets on three carts and also took
aboard two peddlers Bess took a liking to. They was each half
blind and consequently had thrown their lots together, figuring
on making one proper man between them. Threading a needle
would have taxed their abilities, but they professed themselves
keenly interested in knotting one sheet to another, dog collars
being not much in demand that day, and that task they performed well enough. We was fashioning a big tampon, you see,
bunching and tying the looped sheets to a towrope, a bit like
making a paper rose.

By the time we brought the tampon to the building, there
was more carts and horses and a sizable crowd of swabbers as-
sembled. It was astonishing how many of us, myself included,
had kept our old sanitaries. Only sentiment could account for
it, as napkin coats were hardly the latest thing, as could be
proved by the frankly astonished looks of the gawpers. Those as
didn't have sanitaries had thrown on heaps of old nightgowns

all on top of each other, by which—from how they had matching pink collars and cuffs—I surmised another failed business-
man would have a bit of meat to throw in the pot tonight,
thanks to Big Bess. It was a beautiful sight in the blue light of
evening, the company all got up in white gowns, like we was
going off to bed.

We hooked on our lanterns and went up the ladders the firemen had put up to the walls, what were just long enough to
reach above the blood level, though not to reach the roof where
there might have been a door. I personally knocked in the first
window and I must confess I enjoyed it. The room was beautifully appointed and the glass crunched and sparkled on the
floor, but I was mostly struck by the smell of blood, which was
strong and old and weakened my legs and brought the feeling
of Sally close at hand. I felt I'd see her behind me if I turned
around, and I was weak enough to try it, but there was only a
young woman in too many nightgowns stepping through the
window like a stout angel. Like almost everyone there she
looked a little familiar and that only made me miss Sally the
more. If they was still alive, why wasn't she?

I forgot all that in towing the tampon up. It was monstrous
heavy and we didn't have the reel to take up the slack and keep
us from losing the ground we gained. We just ganged up on the
rope and pulled and pulled until the corridor was full and we
was backed up all the way to the stairwell. That was all right,
though, because we figured down the stairwell was the only
way to thread the tampon through the building. We was in luck
that it was the grand spiral kind what has a sizable hole down
the middle.

Once we got the tampon in there wasn't much to do for a

while. We let the tampon down gradual like we used to, and while the sheets wicked up the flow we sat around on Mr. Strick's furniture, feeling precious silly in our sanitaries, and shy with one another. But as soon as the first floor drained far enough, we trooped down. It was a curious sight, the noble oak tables with blood washing around their turned legs, the stained paintings flopping out of their frames. In blood up to our boot tops, we set to work. You might think it would be easy to swab down a room what is basically a box, but you'd not be reckoning with molded plaster ceilings—cupids and drapery in one room, fleur-de-lys in another, and seashells the length of the hall. Wiping cupid's bum and dabbing blood clots out of roses is fiddly work and not exactly in my line. We made our own decisions on what was needful and if the occasional secretary pulled open a drawer and found it full of blood in weeks to come, well, just say we wasn't accustomed to office work. The plaster never did lose its pink tinge.

Everything worked out more or less the way Bess and I had figured; we ran out of sheets at about street level, but then it was an easy thing to drag the used tampon out the door, little by little, using winches and our own backs and those of the horses. We had to take it apart and divide it among the carts. What an unholy mess the uncaulked carts made going down the street! We all took a break while the dockworkers Bess had lined up wrung out the sheets over the Thames. Then we had the whole thing to do over in the underground parts until the whole building was stinking and pink but drained of blood. We tipped our hats to the cement pourers going in to make a giant stopper out of Mr. Strick's marble vaults and stepped out into the dawn. There was already a crowd gathered to cheer us home.

I rinsed out my napkin coat—old habits—and then fell into bed and slept until Bess knocked the next evening. I suppose she knows me pretty well, because she wouldn't let me be, just sat kicking her heels until I got dressed. The pub was given over exclusively to us that night, what had a right to celebrate, for the next day we was cordially invited to shake the hands of the mayor, and the money was as good as in the bank. Everyone was rubbing shoulders and making a good deal of noise. I tried to explain to Bess that I was in a contemplating mood, but Bess pushed me through the crowd and cleared a seat for me. Someone stuck a glass in my hand. Bess had disappeared. One corner of the room was singing one of the carols, and another corner was singing a different one. There was at least two more corners and dozens of songs to go. The woman across the table from me raised her glass to me and said something hearty what I couldn't make out. I smiled and drank her health. I started feeling better.

A little later Bess's ugly, earnest face tunneled up to me through the substantial bums—we was none of us tiny anymore—and someone she had in tow was thrust at me. It was the woman had come up the ladder right after me. She had puzzling eyes, tabby-cat color, but with a star of smoke gray 'round the pupil. I recognized them this time. "You're my tiddler!" says I.

"I'm twenty-four years old," she said. "You stuck pins in my feet."

"Oh well," said I, "you was a bit prim about getting your hands messy."

"I'm not prim now," says she, and sits down on my knee, causing me to put down my glass extremely sudden.

"No," I agreed. Somebody across the table shrieked as the

forward edge of my bitter reached her lap. I am not an ardent person, ordinarily, and my feelings embarrassed me. "Would you like some pot roast?" I said.

"Maybe you could wear your sanitaries one more time," she said.

"You shock me," said I.

We went home at once.

That's my story, and I'm not telling you any more. Good day, sir, and good luck with your book.

MILK

The Greeks divided creation into four elements: earth, air, fire, and milk. Of these, milk is the friendliest, the closest to our hearts. Why does milk fall from the sky to fill our cupped hands? Why do the sweet white rivers roll into the sour sea and never run dry? The answer is obvious: the sky loves us.

Description: Physical Characteristics

(from *The Sky Writer's Phrasebook*)

- the soft ivory clouds were unexpectedly generous above the crisp horizon line
- there was the merest suggestion of nubile curves behind the veil of mist
- budding from the exquisite arc of the sky were tiny clouds of that piquant profile so admired by the French
- the thin air flared into a firm, high-perched cumulonimbus

Where does milk come from? It comes from all around. We drink milk, and when we breathe, tiny milk particles float out into the air. Dogs and cats, shrews and elephants: all mammals exhale milk vapor. The milk in the air collects in clouds; when the sky loves us enough, it rains. After the clouds have dropped their load, they drift back to the sea to replenish themselves. Then they set out over the land again to look for us.

The sea stretches as far as the eye can see. Here in the north its sour smell is only a pleasant tang in the air. Inside its soft, wrinkled skin, the white wave swells. It mounts, still dry, and stands off the beach like an albino animal. Then the skin splits over the crest of the wave and peels back, and out of it leaps the pristine arc. Like a snake shedding in one passionate shrug, the glossy body falls out of its torn skin onto the beach. Papery shreds of discarded skin blow up over the dunes and snag in the twisted cypress trees; we northerners call these "ghosts."

The milk of the northern sea tastes stronger than rain milk, and it is harder to digest, but potable. Travel south, however, and the scene changes. A vast plaque of curdled milk covers the sea. This curd stills all but the most energetic swells, and supports not only extravagant pink, green, and black molds but fields of grass and even the occasional shrub or small tree, as well as vagrant populations of mice, geckos, frogs, and mongooses. One may even see the occasional pilgrimage of the smaller herd animals risking a sea voyage in search of new pastures. Clouds can replenish themselves here only in those vast permanent holes in the curd where the whales surface to breathe.

For large ships, passage through these parts requires a sharp prow known as a butter knife, which can slice through the curd and let it peel smoothly off to either side, although the locals employ a sort of sled, drawn by quick-stepping wing-clipped ducks bred for wide, flat feet. Indeed, locals resent the cargo boats and tankers, and have successfully introduced legislation to confine them to standard routes, so that the mess of curdled-milk floes and butterbergs they leave in their wake do not make the fishing grounds impassable for local traffic.

Fishermen carve holes in the curd and drop their lines in the milk below. They don't seem to mind the stench of sour milk, which would fell a landlubber. It is an easy living: life teems in the dark, secret milk under the rubbery mantle. But a white sea under a white sky is a dazzling sight, and many fishermen suffer from milk blindness. Fishermen sometimes weep over their catch, amazed by the colors slithering into a monochrome world. This is a common thing and not looked down upon.

Description: Color

(from *The Sky Writer's Phrasebook*)

quartz, moonstone, ivory, cream, alabaster, opal, magnolia, vanilla, chalk, oyster, lily, eggshell, ecru

The lucky fisherman who has his eyesight can sometimes watch the rebirth of a cloud.

A cloud that has dropped its milk is a very airy being, practically invisible and by most measures, no longer alive. The dry cloud skin blows around helplessly. Sometimes you will find one snagged in a hedge or wrapped around a television antenna, but these soon disintegrate. The lucky ones are blown out to sea up north or, in the south, into a whale's breathing hole or a ship's tumbled wake. If our watchful mariner is close enough he may see the frail husk sink onto the bosom of a wave. Miraculously, it trembles erect. The translucent skin fills with milk. The shape is tugged this way and that as it fills. It staggers, then grows plump and firm. Within minutes, the wraith has leapt rebodied into the sky.

If the sky expresses its love in milk, then clouds are its organs of expression. Tender impulses form minute thickenings in the tissue of the sky. These lumps grow, incubated by the heat of the sun and kneaded by wind currents. When a critical mass is reached the cloud growth stops. There is a pause. Now something amazing happens. Inside the cloud, tiny lobes and lobules begin to form, grow, and divide. They multiply at an astonishing rate. No further matter is required; the most enormous clouds you have seen are spun, like cotton candy, from a gluey lump no bigger than a baby's clenched fist.

A cloud is a milk-secreting organ. This formless glandular swelling is covered on the lower part or belly of the cloud with minute pores where the milk ducts open. The cloud is not an intelligent life-form, but it does have a primitive muscle system that responds involuntarily to stimulation by stiffening and, if it is engorged, dropping its milk. Clouds are almost entirely made up of milk; that is why they are white. (We, too, are more than 90 percent milk. Though that small proportion of solid matter is enough to make us opaque and colorful, it is well to remember that we are literally intelligent clouds; we have relatives in the sky.) Some clouds have a darker pigment on their rain-bearing underbelly or aureole. This darkening indicates the milk is ready to drop.

The cloud is made up of a fine, branching network of deli-

cate conduits and reservoirs, loosely gathered inside a porous
skin. During lactation or "raining," the cells contract rhythmically and squeeze the milk down the ducts to minute pores in
the skin, where raindrops form. The cloud wrings itself dry, and
as it does so its pigmentation fades, the white drains from its
body, until the cloud is transparent and nearly invisible.

Need I mention that fogs are not clouds? Still, many people
mix them up. Without wishing to enter the fray, I must register
my firm opinion that fogs, which have neither skins nor ducts,
are no more than listless bands of milk droplets that have not
yet found their place in a cloud. These shapeless congeries are
entirely different from those low-flying clouds with which they
are often conflated due to that fallacious but oft-repeated rule
of thumb, *clouds up, fog down.* Why is it so difficult to accept
that while some clouds, true, prefer the upper atmosphere,
other, homelier clouds are moved to shuffle along the ground?
Are we humans (or "walking clouds," as I like to call us) so different?

Sick clouds will often go to earth. If you find a cloud quivering in a field and it does not take flight when you approach it,
palpate it gently to see if it is still cool to the touch, and whether
it springs back when poked. A cystic cloud will feel hot, dry,
and hard. The immediate danger is that the cloud will pop. If
the sickness has progressed this far, there is only one recourse:
a sterilized poker must be thrust through the cloud. A cloud
thus forcibly deprived of its milk will be traumatized, but it is
the only way to save it.

If the cloud is hot but still soft, cover it with a warm, damp
towel to keep it moist and help open its clogged pores. Now you
must gently rock it onto its side, so that you can sponge its aureole in a gentle rotating motion. Croon to the cloud. Small

peeping cries seem to help the cloud relax. Don't be alarmed if its milk begins to gush, but draw off the towel and let the cloud rise. You have probably saved its life.

There are also hysterical clouds that show every sign of releasing milk, but remain dry; these malfunctioning clouds are suffering a kind of insanity, if it is proper to speak of insanity with regard to beings that show no signs of what we recognize as cognition. Nonetheless, we cannot help but anthropomorphize these clouds, which seem all the more like us in their confusion. We sympathize involuntarily with their "pride" and their "distress."

Other *seeming* clouds drop a tasteless, cold, unnourishing liquid. Once, this liquid was considered poisonous, but now we know it is chillingly devoid of properties, for good or ill. These are not true clouds at all, but the skins of clouds hijacked by non-milk-based fluids, and compelled to take their fraudulent cargo along the sky road with the other, real clouds. This liquid—this milkless milk, this *abstraction*—has its admirers. I fear them. Addictive? No, this "water" is not addictive. Water rebuffs need as it rebuffs passion, love, simple tenderness. Even politeness is too warm for it.

Water is modern, oh yes, cruelly so. It is the fuel of a streamlined future. Weaned from milk, we will step forth as autocrats of the nursery, pooh-poohing our teddy bears. This love that makes us tremble with gratitude, our betrothal to the ardent sky, will give way to a pallid aestheticism, the motivator of weekend watercolorists and the peddlers of picture windows to country homemakers. As children we lay on the grass and opened our mouths to be fed; we knew the sky would not overlook us, and it did not. In the watery new world, we will seek shelter from the rain—characterless drops that fall without reason from a sky without feeling. If that day ever comes, let the traduced clouds drop their cargo, let it never stop. Forty days and forty nights may it rain, until there is water, water everywhere, and not a drop to drink. I will drown thirsty, with the taste of milk on my tongue.

Description: Physical Characteristics

(from *The Sky Writer's Phrasebook*)

- the sky was dark and insolent and, despite 100 percent visibility, untouchable
- our gaze dropped from the smoldering blue—to the mounded, immaculate tops of the clouds—to their swollen underbellies
- behind a modest cloud ceiling, the sky was all thermal churning and moist gradients
- we sensed the sensuality throbbing behind the crisp lace of the stratus layer
- there was a maddening hint of arrogance about the cirrus clouds so carelessly displayed above the rich skirting of fog

It is possible to compute how much the sky loves us. This may be expressed in a number of forms, namely: (1) the milk pressure m, which is that part of total atmospheric pressure p that is exerted by milk; (2) the relative humidity m/ma, which is the percentage ratio of the existing milk pressure to the maximum possible (saturation) milk pressure a as determined by the degree of tenderness felt by the sky (it is to be noted that saturation milk pressure is a function of love alone, lowering exponentially with the degree of passion, that is, the more love the sky feels for us, the less milk it will hold back); (3) the dew point, which is the intensity of romantic feeling to which the air must be raised, under the existing milk pressure, to reach lactation.

The old superstition that people born in a milkstorm have special powers to bring down milk has almost attained respectability. Some mayors of milk-belt cities have even hired old-fashioned milk doctors to massage the clouds and sing down the milk. The barbaric custom of firing missiles through clouds, on the other hand, has been almost eradicated by fierce public opinion. Even countries whose skies do not love them very much have by and large been persuaded not to ambush with bullets or arrows the few clouds that visit them, and to adopt gentler ways. Famous milk doctors have made well-publicized trips to these loveless parts to sing milk songs and call the clouds. Results have not been spectacular, but it takes time to woo such austere skies as these.

Action: Attraction, Desire

(From *The Sky Writer's Phrasebook*)

- the west held our ardent gaze with dark defiance, but a rising excitement stained the east with a rush of pink
- the rosy peaks stiffened
- the very air seemed electrified
- The Coriolis force had the sky in its grip
- the clouds tingled/prickled/burned against the silky wind belt

- turbulent diffusion spread warmth through the entire body
of the sky, until it could not suppress a clap of thunder

In the books it seems simple. "Red sky at night, sailor's delight." One thing leads to another, a "delicious shudder" goes through the "welkin," and pretty soon you're swimming in milk. We are thrilled by the sky on the page. But the sky overhead makes us a little uncomfortable, with its stillness and its expectancy. We write *the sky is beautiful here* on the backs of postcards that prove it, but when we walk to the mailbox, we keep our eyes on the ground. We buy blow-up plastic clouds and stay indoors.

Once we all knew how to make love to the sky. Watch a baby kneading, sucking, mouthing. In our earliest instincts, we can trace the lineaments of the ancient art. But these are uncertain times, and we no longer trust ourselves. I shall venture, then, to provide some guidance.

First, the sky loves us. It will shower us with milk whatever we do, as a baby is cuddled even when it cries, and does not need to flirt or doll itself up to get its chin chucked. We are afraid of looking foolish, or needy. We are afraid of doing something wrong. Let us abandon these fears.

There is vast room for variation in the love act. True, it is just this latitude that terrifies beginners. "If whips are required, bring me a whip"—they say— "of the proper gauge, and teach me how to use it; if it is the overhead serve, fine, or a flamenco step, I will undertake to learn it, but don't send me into the backyard with nothing in my hands, and the voluptuous sky spread above me!" Whips may be used, certainly, and racquets, and staccato foot-stamping. So may wind socks, ribbons, balloons; so may textual analysis and fly-tying. In brief, there's no end to the techniques that will please the sky, if undertaken with feeling, so let us start with the basics, and leave the rest to individual taste.

Go outside. You don't know how to make the sky notice you? Don't worry. The sky already touches you. Your least movement is a caress.

Crook your finger. Feel a slight resistance? Try it again. A coy reluctance, shading almost at once into a gay giving way? Reach forward boldly and squeeze the sky. You will have to get used to the texture of it; the sky is so soft, it accepts everything you do. We're not used to that much freedom. Open your mouth and let the sky slip in, then press it back out. Now blow gently. Feel a breeze? Run your fingers through it. Press your thumbs into the sky, then insert your fingers, one at a time, slowly stretching the space you have made. Don't be afraid of hurting the sky. Pull steadily up and back. Molecular viscosity will increase. Tell the sky how pretty it is. Wiggle your fingers slightly. Let the sky bear down on you, but press back.

When you see the clouds gathering, almost anything you do will give pleasure. Now you don't need to worry about being too rough. The aforementioned whips and racquets may be brought out. Find the sky's sweet spot and you can thrash away with all your might. Now is the time to let the traditional milk songs come rolling boldly forth. If you're no singer, never mind! Wordless cries are just as bewitching to the sky.

It is almost dew point. Forget technique. The sky loves you. The clouds are massed above you. Do you want milk? Just cup your hands, and tell the sky *I love you.*

Action: Milkfall

(from *The Sky Writer's Phrasebook*)

- the sky surrendered utterly, and knew the flooding of uncontrollable pleasure
- the sweet agony wrung a moist effluvium from the sky's throbbing center
- we shut our eyes as the warm drops drenched our upturned faces

FAT

I'm afraid things have gone to pot around here since you left. Cadbury has buried the remote control and I've let myself go. I know you think I should keep my nose clean and return to my studies; that's all very well, but I have less and less room to move. I could barely get out of bed this morning for the weight on the coverlet, though mind you there's no particular need to go to bed to go to sleep, now everything's so squishy.

Have I embarrassed you? Face it, Boney, fat falls. In the neatest homes. In palaces and hovels! But we don't talk about it. Only a few greasy, fly-by-night presses put out the occasional pamphlet saying what we already know, just to *épater les* uptight. That means you, Jack. But once we read them to each other like pornography.

"Let a house be scraped down to the last layer of paint the night before, it will be buttered by morning; leave it for a week and fat will round every contour. Vacation homes fill with fat; fat bursts the boards from old barns, leaving a barn-shaped block of suet to stand until the warm weather. Fat comes of its own accord, clogging chimneys and closets, stealthily amassing behind the drapes. Isn't it time we admitted we all have it? Let me go one step further: that we need it? It's our food!"

You loved that bit. "It's our food!" you crooned, stuffing a gooey finger in my mouth. You were holding the page open with your elbow. " 'We live on it'—now swallow, there's a good girl—'but we don't discuss it; a vast mutual deception that people of other cultures find hard to understand. Babies love fat and are forgiven for it, but toddlers are sent to their rooms to eat, while adults lick the undersides of chairs, or floss the balustrades, in strictest privacy, and shudder to see foreigners run a finger between the sofa cushions to find a snack. Their houses wobble and shine. Ours are dry, every mitered joint painstakingly scraped clean.' " But not mine. Not anymore, Jack.

You were the one who wanted a traditional wedding. I still have the article you handed me by way of asking. "Like Carnival, the cataclysm of marriage occasions a temporary inversion of values; the private is publicized, the unspoken spoken, the degraded is raised up. The bride and groom are left alone to fast. They allow fat to form on their naked bodies; this is augmented on the eve of the wedding by the bridesmaids and best man, who dab on pats of it until the couple is encased in towering masses, hers a sphere, his a cone. These wobbling, glistening behemoths are rolled on trolleys down the wide aisle. (Many urban churches no longer possess the high ceilings this ceremony requires.) In the center of each mass hangs the naked body like a larva." While I read, you blushed and fiddled with the ring.

"Members of the audience fling themselves upon the couple as they pass, vying for scoops of the fat, which is deemed lucky. In olden days this was a time for feasting; now the blobs are col-

lected by church functionaries with trash bags, or left on news-
papers placed under each chair. By the time the bride and
groom reach the altar, they are much reduced (these were days
of large weddings) and their faces bared. Our modern kiss was
once the first bite of spousal fat. Bride and groom are swept off
to a private chamber, where they lick each other clean, a
process that may take hours. Engorged, they mate, then sleep.
This ceremony, so seldom performed these days, is even more
binding now, for having shared this distressing transaction,
husband and wife may be bound for life by mutual embarrass-
ment."

And you, Boney, with whom I shared those sacred rites, you
pretend to find me unclean—you who took me for better or for
worse, for saturated or unsaturated, who reveled in the ineffa-
ble textures of my lard, and whispered foul words to me: *but-
tery, oleaginous, pinguid, adipose*. Whatever you are doing now,
you are a phony, Mr. Sprat.

I am writing to tell you I'm still eating. I have seen the sun
rise at fatfall and felt the hot blobs pepper my thighs. My dog
swims in the center of the living room, his poop hangs above
my sofa; I am letting my house fill up. I will wear a poultice on
my forehead, and seal my eyes with buttons of fat. Surely these
gestures deserve some response. I spread the fat on the lawn
and stroke it onto the lilies. Tulip cups are plugged with it.
Roses are beautiful blurs in the banks. Astonished bugs and
mice and cats get stuck in the suet. It will not harm them.

While you keep dry in your house of shell and aluminum, in
that fat-free land behind the sun, click beetles will telegraph
my feats to you, and your toe bones will rattle as you wonder at
me. Yes, my fat hat is as tall as your saguaros! Yes, my gown is
oleomargarine and hydrogenated. One of these days I will set a

match to all this, and then, dear Bones, though my flame may not outshine your sun, my smoke will put it out. I am painting trees with domestic Crisco, dear. I am covering the car, and see, what fun, I am rolling fat balls, big, bigger, biggest. What for? Meet Fatty the Fatman!

I can't help it, I was so lonely. He is not much like you—so rounded, so comfortable, so very relaxed. I could sink into him. In fact, I have—I tried to sit on his lap yesterday. I found myself inside him! He didn't mind, Boney, so you needn't shake your rattletrap head.

I have snipped your signature off your last letter—it was months ago, Jack—and poked it into his head with a pencil. The hole closed up on its own.

I've brought him inside. We watch TV. The set is buried, but we can see the moving shapes, and the blue light. In our bliss, it's all we need.

I am selling ties made of fat. Ties, and aprons, and mittens. I stamp them with the image of the Fatman. They're doing very well!

No, of course they are not doing well. Nothing is doing well. I suppose I sleep well, except I set the alarm six months ago, and it goes off twice a day, somewhere deep in the fat. I can't reach it to turn it off, I can't find it, I can't bother to find it. The fat is piling above my chimney. It piles, and piles, like an upward icicle, a stalagmite, and then it topples. And then once again it piles and piles. The roof is covered with fallen piles, the mound rises higher and higher. Birds pass over the house and are seized in mid-flight. They stick there, batting their wings if they still can, until they fall into lassitude and despair. Eventually they will probably die, though surrounded by food. My dog is not so stupid; he eats his way away from his shit, and bores a shitty tunnel toward the door. Boney-o's gone hunting, his knees a-clacking, his ribs going rat-a-tat-tat, and an oboe for a nose. Long white bones and the rest all gone.

The pit slipped out of the apricot and went for a walk. Good riddance!

You always warned me to scrape behind my ears and spoon between my toes, to squeegee my back and the closet doors, to wipe behind the organ and irrigate the jambs. Now I mortify myself. Frosted all over with fat, like a despairing cake, I circumnavigate the yard at a crawl. The house is the center of my orbit. Here I go, 'round and 'round, crawling, and I don't really know why, except that someone has probably set me at it, hence this feeling of obligation and even, yes, an obscure satisfaction, not pleasure of course, but a dog's satisfaction at obeying orders. Whose? Must be yours, Boney-o. Oh, I can see you now, adjusting your cuffs, crossing your narrow ankles, not looking at me as you remind me of your hopes for me, which I will never live up to. "Up to which I will never live," you bark. You have a cane hooked over your elbow. What a fop you are, Mr. Clean. And what a caricature. Yes, maybe I'm getting muddled, mixing you up with a character in a storybook.

In any case I'm growing uneasy with the idea that you ordered me to crawl around the house like this, "frosted all over with fat, like a despairing cake." As if you could come up with something like that! No, I'm probably doing it to spite you. I'm wearing my dressing gown, the one you hate, with the roses. All my other clothes are lost. Why do you hate this dressing gown? I know, it's the roses, big as cabbages, shameless as a beaver shot. They cheer me up.

The little birds squeak from their weird perch. Maybe after all they'll be OK, the sun will melt the fat on their wings and they'll go flapping off to their babies. No, I can hear you saying, some things just aren't meant to work out, pull yourself together.

I know what you want, Boney-o, don't think I don't see it. When I'm as thin as you wish I were I'll be a skeleton.

When I get tired of crawling, I go into the house, and when I get tired of the house, I crawl. Since nobody has commanded me to crawl, I can set my own hours and even take days off if I want to, though usually I like to get some crawling done every day. The point is, it's up to me; that's the advantage of being self-employed. I sometimes think I'm setting a new standard for crawling, or as I sometimes call it for the novelty, creeping; then I remember I'm the only one doing it. It doesn't matter anyway. Whether I crawl with particular intricacy, or with irony, or with girlish artlessness, I'm only pleasing myself, not that I shouldn't please myself; in fact if I wait for someone to wade into the garden to drop a medal over my neck for freestyle creeping, I'll wait a long time.

It's interesting, though, that there are aesthetic satisfactions to be had in, loosely speaking, crap: the rattle of phlegm in the throat, the shine and firmness of some turds, much nicer than the raggedy look of others, and fat, too, that offal, is sometimes, oh, marvelous—a trembling, fragile, cream-colored gateau—while sometimes, I'll just say (to spare your sensibilities), less marvelous. For example when it has hair and sweepings mixed with it. Or has gone a bit curdy and horn-colored on the exposed parts. But I did not mean to describe it.

Crawling, I have made a circular track around the house,

with built-up edges. My dressing gown smoothes it into a glossy, even surface, which is a never-ending pleasure to look upon, shining a short distance ahead of me to where the curve cuts it off from view. Though sometimes Cadbury trots after me and spoils it.

I have had to make a path from the house to the track and so I have just continued this radial line, in accordance with a rather geometrical sense of order, out to the mailbox. From this path I make irregular tracks outward to continue frosting the yard. I have not coated the mailbox, because I am afraid the mailman would not pick up the letters, but I've almost finished the fence and the tree, and of course all the smaller plants are done. I don't expect congratulations, needless to say.

Even though I trowel out wheelbarrow loads of fat from the house, the space inside gets smaller and smaller. I crawl up a sloping tunnel to my cave in the center of the biggest room, the living room. It is a little round hollow like a stomach. Below me I see the vague shape of the couch (itself covered with roses, another bit of gaucherie, no?) and the coffee table. The bookshelves are no longer visible except when the sun shines through the fat. Then I can see everything, though foggily: the colored spines of the books, Cadbury's turds, a pair of my underwear floating like a jellyfish, and a mouse who, like me, has made himself a little round cave with a tunnel leading up to it, and lined the bottom with part of the jacket of my collected Kafka (black and red shreds). It is almost like flying, to float here in the middle of the room, only it is more like being mummified, because my legs are trapped; in fact whenever I stop moving, I begin to melt a little way into the fat, making a cavity shaped precisely like me, as if it were a mold in which I'd hardened, like a candle or a statue. You'd like that, wouldn't you? To be a statue, I mean. So definite, so martial. They might even melt you down for bullets!

Cadbury is in a worse state, for sinking in, because his body heat's higher, though the fur insulates him; still, by morning he's swimming. By morning, too, the tunnel has closed up, but so far it hasn't been too hard to dig my way through again, though once—I was pretty groggy—I tunneled the wrong way and didn't even know it until I hit the kitchen sink. I expect the mouse has the same problem. It's a bond between us.

The windowpanes have popped out, forced from their frames by the fat, and are lying unbroken on the heaps outside, reflecting the sky.

I can no longer fit the Fatman into the house. It is too big a job digging the tunnel wide enough every evening to push him up it, not to mention the disturbing way he sticks to everything. If I'm not careful he might even grow into the house and vice versa, and I will have to dig him out in handfuls, or else there will be nothing left of him but two embalmed carrots and a slip of paper, somewhere in my living room, and only visible on sunny days!

Two carrots, you ask? Why, sir, I blush.

I have left him outside. I smoothed his body into three shining white spheres, so he will look his best. I'm not coming back.

Yes, I'm planning to stay in from now on. In the end, my skeleton will hang here, in the center of a block of lard, beautiful as a bug in amber. One day maybe you will come home. If you want to gather my adorable bones, you will have to eat your way to them. Yes, Mr. Nobody, that's only fair: a second wedding most prodigious. At last, Boney-o, we will each have what we crave, you a skeleton, and I (and this is my revenge) a fat man.

I fell asleep and dreamed I was a candle. A wick ran through me and out the top of my skull, and as it burned the fat level sank in the room. First the crown of my head was bared, with a flame standing above it; then my whole skull, blazing like a jack-o'-lantern. My shoulders freed themselves and my rib cage became a lampshade to the flame in my chest, but when the descending flame reached my pelvis, I woke up.

I was stuck fast! The fat cleaved to my forehead and cheeks, and fluttered against my nostrils. A thin, constant stream of warm oil was running into my mouth and down my throat. I forced my eyes open. It was morning, the sun was out, the window was closer than the door, and I began to swim, the hardest thing I'd ever done. I wasn't sure I wasn't dreaming. I wasn't sure I was moving; was that my foot I felt? I thought I might be batting my feet, that was something I could do, they had called it the flutter kick when I was learning to swim as a girl, it didn't seem very effective back then, plenty of splash but very little forward movement, much like everything else we do, and it seemed even less effective now, but I did it. My hands, if I could find them, I could pull in to my sides, and then slide them, very craftily, with a minimum of fuss, up along my body, past my ears, and then shoot them forward together. And as I pull them down, flutter kicking, I will inch forward.

Shoot forward, pull down, flutter kick. I think I am moving; I might not be. I'll know by the mouse. That's it, I'll steer by the mouse, poor little carcass, it will be my North Star, I'll set my astrolabe to it. Musculus the Mouse Star. Verminus?

Why does no one help me? Funny, that, when I think about

it. Shouldn't there be a policeman around, at a time like this? Or a handsome policewoman, stretching the long arm of the law through the window to tow me out? Maybe nobody knows I'm here, nobody saw me, crawling through the roses in my rosy robe, 'round and 'round. A rose is a rose is a rose. I would accept a helping hand from the stalwart Miss Stein. Shoot forward, pull down . . . I close my eyes, so that when I open them again I will be amazed at how far I've gotten. Instead I'm amazed at how close I am to being exactly where I started.

How is it possible nobody saw me? Of course, I lied about the ties, nobody buys ties made of fat, nobody wants to look at fat, least of all my fat, if they want to look at fat they can look at their own.

I am inching past the sofa. The window is at 19 degrees off due Mouse. I will get there, after I swim through twenty-seven pancakes and a lake of syrup, and those tigers that turned into butter. I could eat my way out, but that would take too long.

If I could gather my resources for a really good fart, it might propel me some distance, but I am becalmed. Mouse to starboard. Somebody must have seen me, if I was there; of course I was there. Boney's the one who's missing, even if he does get all the mail. I used to throw it in the closet, when I could reach the closet, throw not being the right word, *poke* or *stuff* rather. Then after a while I just put the mail on the pile in the garden. I looked on it as a rustic touch, a sort of haycock of letters. I covered that with fat too, and each new letter, as it came. They saw me, I guess, and at the same time didn't see me. Who notices the fat lady? In an hour I will reach the windowsill. Thank God the glass is gone.

Musculus before me. I will take him with me, to commemorate our voyage together. I carve out a ball around him and hug

it to my stomach like a football player. Now I must swim with
just one arm and the after all much underrated flutter kick. I
press my eyelids open and I can see green, blue, yellow light
coming in from outside.

I touch the windowsill!

At last my head pops through.

I lie still for a while, poking out the window. Mostly I am
breathing, and spitting clots of melting lard. Despite the fat
plugging my ears, I hear the birds—the flying ones, and the sad
ones that are stuck in my tower. Clouds are running across the
sky. It is funny the way an accident happens, I am calling it an
accident though we both know better, and for a while one has
a purpose. I felt important for a little while, charged with the
task of saving myself, inventing a system of navigation and
brushing off my flutter kick. I will probably remember that as
the best time of my life. But now that I've arrived at my desti-
nation (which a short time ago was precious and almost unat-
tainable), how disappointing: I'm in an ordinary and slightly
ridiculous position, halfway out of a window. It is worth philos-
ophizing about, Boney.

So I won't rest on my laurels. Now that my house is unin-
habitable, I must build an igloo. The first thing I do, after I
climb down, is trace a circle on the ground. The first block I lay
must be the one that encases Musculus. I hew it into a brick and
place it on the circumference. Now I have my plan, I am zeal-
ous. Of course, I cut blocks in which there are roses, beautifully
embalmed. I am saddened to find Cadbury, too, buried in a
deep bank, and I cut a large block around him and place him
opposite Musculus, at the entrance. Near the tree I find fat full
of ants and I cut a block of it, and of a batch into which a cater-
pillar has fallen. I lay my blocks systematically; I work in a cir-

cle, creeping around my igloo, and when I have used all the blocks, I creep up to the roof of the house—not as difficult as it sounds, because the drifts come up to the eaves—and I push over the fat pole and cut blocks full of birds, and from these I make the ceiling, standing on Fatman's lap. Did I forget to mention I built the igloo around him? I take off my robe, bundle it outside, and seal the door with one last block.

I am eating the Fatman. It is our marriage ceremony. But when I am done, I shall find myself married to nobody.

Jack, I must have eaten your signature without noticing it. Oops! I eat one of the carrots, but keep the other.

The day I finished dinner, spring came. It was an uncommonly hot day for March. I was single and exceedingly fat. The igloo had become a luminous dome. The animals sealed in every block stood out as clear as cameos. Cadbury was on his back, his muzzle pointing up. The ants were dotted elegantly through their block. Some of the birds were in attitudes of flight, some were hunched into the shape of endives. I could see where the sun stood over me: it blazed through the fat. The blaze climbed the dome, and the dome heated up, and when the shadow of the birds fell directly over me, I felt a hot drop hit my ankle.

It started to rain hot fat. I turned onto my stomach and let the molten drops hit my back, my thighs, my ass. Soon I lay in a warm bath of clear oil, on a bed of grass and pebbles. The level was rising, but as the oil poured down, fissures were forming at the base of the walls and between blocks, through which it was running away. The igloo grew brighter and more transparent, a thin, blazing shell, and then it wobbled and collapsed in on me. All the trapped oil ran off into the grass.

I sat up. All around me animals were struggling up, alive!

The birds staggered around, spreading out their gunky wings. The sun seemed to shine on us with the specific intention of licking us clean. We moved our limbs in wonder like cripples faith-healed. I lay back in the slick and smiled. There were roses everywhere. There went Musculus. Cadbury was prancing. The first birds tried their wings. I was shining like a gold medal.